The Roommate

"I said, what are you doing? Have you been going through my things?" Margot demanded.

Backing away, Danni shook her head mutely.

"Answer me," said Margot harshly. "Have you been going through my things?"

"No! No, I — I . . ." Danni looked wildly around.

Margot picked up the knife. "I saw you with this in your hand. It's mine. Don't touch anything of mine unless you ask."

NIGHTMARE HALL

The Roommate

Diane Hoh

SCHOLASTIC

Scholastic Children's Books,
Scholastic Publications Ltd,
7-9 Pratt Street, London NW1 OAE, UK

Scholastic Inc.,
555 Broadway, New York, NY 10012-3999, USA

Scholastic Canada Ltd,
123 Newkirk Road, Richmond Hill,
Ontario, Canada L4C 3G5

Ashton Scholastic Pty Ltd,
PO Box 579, Gosford, New South Wales,
Australia

Ashton Scholastic Ltd,
Private Bag 92801, Penrose, Auckland,
New Zealand

First published in the US by Scholastic Inc., 1993
First published in the UK by Scholastic Publications Ltd, 1994

Text copyright © Nola Thacker 1993

ISBN: 0 590 55522 7

Printed and bound in Great Britain by BPC Paperbacks Ltd

Prologue

Underwear.
Socks.
Shirts.
A photograph of the parents.

Yes. That was a nice touch. Or maybe not. Oh well. It could always be ditched upon arrival.

A whole new life was ahead. That's what everyone always said about college. You couldn't believe everything everyone told you, of course.

Because people lied to you. Made you promises they never intended to keep. Watched you all the time to see if you believed them. If you trusted them.

But you were smarter than they were. You had them all fooled. They were the crazy, trusting ones. Not you.

Never you.

Pants.

Shoes.

Packing for college. Neatly. Organized. Obeying the list the college sent. No hot plates. No popcorn poppers allowed in rooms. A college dorm room wasn't a kitchen. So you didn't bring kitchen utensils into it.

Except one.

Wipe off that last little smidgen of blood.

There.

Smile at your reflection in the beautiful shining blade.

Perfect.

Now.

Lift the underwear at the bottom of the suitcase and slide it in. Lovingly. Carefully, carefully. Because you are packing your best friend. The keen, sweet, understanding instrument of your freedom. The most important thing of all.

The knife.

Chapter 1

Clothes covered the room: both beds, both desks, both chairs, spilled out of three suitcases and one trunk on the floor.

The chests of drawers were still empty. So were both closets.

The girl was wearing a towel.

"I know you're here *some*where," she said aloud, bending over to shift the mountain of clothes on one bed. Shirts and underwear and scarves and hats began to cascade off the bed onto the floor.

"Hey," the girl said. She made a frantic dive and came up with a handful of clothes.

Her towel slipped.

Dropping the underwear to grab the towel, she said one word, loudly and firmly.

Someone gasped. Someone else began to laugh.

She looked up.

Two girls stood in the doorway of suite 2AB in the Quad dormitory. One girl was tall and dramatic-looking with a mane of honey-colored hair, unusual gray-blue eyes that turned slightly down at the corners, pale skin the color of moonlight, and a smile curving her generous mouth. The other was even taller, with a long crop of straight dark hair pulled severely back, pale skin the color of too many days inside a library, round green eyes behind a pair of glasses held together at one temple with a paper clip, and a stubborn upper lip, at the moment tucked disapprovingly into her lower lip.

Lacey Sakurada began to smile. She pulled the towel into place and repeated the word. The lion-maned girl smiled back and raised her eyebrows. The mousey one gave an agitated squeak.

"Hey," said Lacey.

"Hi," said the smiling girl. "I'm Danni Spelling."

They both looked at the mousey girl. She gave Lacey a scared look and said in a breathless whisper, "Maureen Ross."

"I'm Lacey," said Lacey. "As in underwear . . . as in *where* did I put my panties?"

Lacey bent over to inspect the pile of clothes

she'd just dropped, ignoring the precariously slipping towel. "Aha!" she said, straightening up a moment later to triumphantly brandish a wispy bit of pink silk and lace.

"Oh!" said Maureen. Slow, dull red began to flood her cheeks.

"I was afraid I was going to have to go through my entire college career without wearing any." Lacey addressed Maureen as she shimmied on the scrap of silk she'd declared was underwear.

Lacey pulled a billowing shirt of thin silk over her head, and after another search, produced a pair of baggy black pants. Then she turned to face herself in the mirror above the bureau and tilted her head to one side, studying the reflection of her own laughing, restless face. What she saw apparently pleased her, from the smooth skin with the faintly golden glow to the almost shockingly short hair to the humorous brown eyes that turned up at the corners. She smiled at her reflection and turned back to face the other two girls.

"So?" asked Lacey. "You're what? The suite-mates? Although personally, I wouldn't call this dump a suite. Two rooms connected by a bathroom that's not even a full bath — I mean, no way is a toilet and sink a real bathroom, no matter what the Salem U. student housing brochures said, right? Especially since we still have to go all the way down the hall to the showers — anyway, where was I? Oh, yeah, I think old Salem U. is stretching it to call this a suite, don't you?"

Maureen turned even redder, swallowed hard, and then in a strangled voice said, "Y-yes. I mean, no. Not exactly."

Lacey picked up a glass container of Body Shop lipgloss and began to lovingly smooth translucent color on her lips with her forefinger. "It's *not* a trick question," she told Maureen.

Danni smiled at Maureen reassuringly and then addressed Lacey. "I'm your suitemate," Danni said. "But whoever my roommate is in 2B hasn't arrived yet."

Once again they both looked at Maureen. She rushed into speech: "Ah. Uh, well, I, uh . . . what I mean is . . ." Maureen pushed her glasses up her nose and squared her thin shoulders resolutely. Then she stuck out her hand awkwardly and walked forward. "Hello, Lacey," she said. "I'm your roommate."

Lacey looked down at Maureen's outstretched hand. She shook her head. "You're kidding, right? Not," Lacey added hastily, "that I have anything against you as a roommate. But I'm like, noisy and messy and stuff like that. You sort of look — the opposite. Yeah, like, the *exact* opposite."

Although it didn't seem possible, Maureen turned even redder. She jerked her hand down and started to back up — and almost fell.

"Whoa!" cried Lacey, catching one of Maureen's flailing arms and helping her to regain her balance.

"I'm awfully sorry. I'm clumsy, I can't help it, I . . ." Maureen ducked her head as if she expected Lacey to hit her.

"Hey, no problem," said Lacey, instantly contrite. "Me and my big mouth. Sometimes I'm just outta control, you know?" She grabbed Maureen's nerveless hand and pumped it up and down with exaggerated enthusiasm. "Roomie! Welcome! And neighbor Danni! Listen, I'm about to go out — this *major* decent guy was helping me carry some of my stuff up until this dragon of a housemother came out of nowhere and said, 'No males allowed in the young ladies' living quarters except during certain hours' and like, expelled him. I can't believe my parents stuck me in an all-girl dorm with these old-fashioned rules! I mean, how out of it can you get? Like nobody does this drill anymore. Anyway, the least I can do is make it up to him, right? But when I get back tonight — I'm pretty sure it'll be tonight — let's talk. Okay? Okay."

Lacey scooped a key and some money from the top of the chest of drawers near her bed. "Later!" she cried, rushing to the door. She waved over her shoulder. "Make yourself at home, Maureen."

The door shut behind her.

The two girls looked at the door and then at each other and Danni began to laugh. "Looks like you're the reform candidate."

"What do you mean?" Maureen had begun disentangling her feet from the clothes. She raised one foot and shook a sheer black bra off of it.

Danni explained, "Maybe you're supposed to be a good influence on Lacey, or something."

Panic showed in Maureen's face. "Oh, I couldn't! I . . ."

"Just a joke, Maureen. Listen, why don't I help you get your stuff up here and organized? I mean, unless your parents are still here?"

Maureen shook her head, looking scared and

close to tears. "I-I told them to go ahead and leave. It wasn't going to get any easier if they stayed."

Obviously a sensitive subject, thought Danni. She nudged Maureen gently toward the door. "I thought I'd never get here, myself," she said. "You wouldn't believe what I had to do! I decided to be brave and come all alone, on my own, you know? But then, I didn't know how to tell the cab driver to get here from the airport."

"You took a *cab*? Alone?" Maureen allowed herself to be guided out the door and down the hall.

"Yeah, well when you have parents whose idea of a good time is traveling to places that are practically not even on the maps, cabs are the least of your worries. Anyway, I got here, and so did you and so did Lacey. So we're just waiting for my mystery roommate."

Talking with determined cheerfulness, Danni managed to persuade Maureen to let her help get her trunk and suitcases and boxes up to the suite without any major crisis. Danni was surprised to discover when she reached for one of the suitcases that Maureen wasn't always as mousey as she'd seemed at first.

"No!" said Maureen sharply, trying to wrest the suitcase from Danni's hands. "I'll take that one!"

"That's all right, Maureen," said Danni. "It's not all that heavy . . ."

"Give it to me," demanded Maureen.

She jerked the suitcase out of Danni's hand, lost her balance and staggered back, dropping it. The suitcase burst open.

Maureen fell to her knees and began to frantically scoop up the contents of the case.

Danni bent over to help.

"No, no!" cried Maureen, waving a hand in front of Maureen's face as if she were trying to hide something from Danni's sight.

Thinking Maureen was embarrassed, Danni said, "Hey, Maureen, it's okay."

"Leave me *alone*," gasped Maureen. She pushed Danni away. "Go . . . go get that box over there."

"Okay, okay," said Danni. She couldn't help wondering . . . what was Maureen hiding?

Chapter 2

At last Danni put a final box on the floor of Maureen and Lacey's room, and straightened up with a sigh of relief. "Whew," she said. "What have you got in these boxes, anyway?"

"Books," answered Maureen.

"Books? Oh. I guess you do need some for college."

But Maureen wasn't listening. She was staring around the room with a terrified expression. "Where do I put everything?" she asked.

"Well, which bed do you want? Whichever one you choose, that means the bookshelf and the desk and the chest of drawers near it are yours, too. Same for the closet."

"I don't know which one Lacey wants!" wailed Maureen. "What if I choose the bed she wants? She'll hate me for the rest of the year."

Danni stifled another sigh. "I bet Lacey doesn't even care. Besides, she told you to make yourself at home, right? And she seems pretty casual about things."

But it took all the cheerful talk Danni had left before she finally convinced Maureen to choose a bed and a chest of drawers and a desk and a closet. *I sound just like one of those mental hospital nurses,* she thought wryly.

"I'm gonna go get started on my stuff," Danni told Maureen at last. "I'll be right through here," she nodded at the bathroom, "if you need anything."

"Th-thanks. Thanks a lot." Maureen looked up and smiled gratefully at Danni. The smile transformed her face. For a moment, she didn't look like a lost kid. She didn't even look like the same person.

Danni was startled. It was as if Maureen were two different people.

But before Danni could say anything, a knock sounded on the door and Maureen's smile was wiped away. "What if it's Lacey?" asked Maureen, her voice rising.

"She *is* your roommate, you know," Danni pointed out. When Maureen didn't answer, Danni said, "Come in!"

A tall, dark-skinned girl with loose curly hair and a patient, world-weary expression pushed the door to room 2A open. "Y'all settling in okay?"

"Just fine," said Danni as Maureen bobbed her head up and down like something on the dashboard of a car.

"Good," said the girl. "I'm Kendra Sydney. I'm your R.A. — also known as your resident advisor — which is Salem University's way of saying I'm the senior assigned to this floor to keep an eye on you lucky first-year students. I'm the one who makes sure y'all don't burn the place down, get lost, or get *too* confused. In exchange for my giving you the benefit of my wisdom and maturity, Salem gives me free room and board. Any questions?"

Trying to sound more assured then she felt, Danni said, "Sounds good to me. I'm Danni Spelling and this is Maureen Ross. So far, we're not lost." Or at, least, *I'm* not, she thought, looking over at Maureen, who was staring in a strange trancelike way at Kendra. "But then, I haven't even left the dorm yet."

Kendra's shrewd brown eyes twinkled knowingly. "You'll get your chance at dinner at the Commons. That's the main campus cafeteria in the Student Center, which is on one side of Salem Commons. There's a smaller dining hall here in the dorm, too. Same menus. Same food." Kendra made a wry face. "But most folks go to the Commons. Meanwhile, if you need anything, let me know. Oh, yeah — we're going to have a house meeting tonight in the Dungeon at eight o'clock."

"The *Dungeon*?" gasped Maureen.

"It's the basement. Wait'll you see it. It runs underneath the whole Quad. The Quad is really four connected dorms, with a courtyard in the center — hence the clever name the Quad. There's a map to the Dungeon on the bulletin board by my door at the end of the hall." Kendra waved her hand vaguely. "The meeting's in the lounge next to the laundry room. See you tonight."

"*Dungeon?*" Maureen repeated weakly as Kendra strode out.

"You know, for the really crazy students," said Danni, laughing.

Maureen didn't laugh. After a moment, Danni stopped laughing and said, "It was a joke, Maureen."

"Oh. Yeah." Maureen smiled mechanically and began to slowly take things out of one of her symmetrically packed suitcases and line them up just so in the drawers.

"Well," said Danni. Was everything Maureen owned in shades of beige and brown? Depressing. Institutional. Maybe Maureen had parents who believed in being practical. Maybe they'd even sewed labels in all of Maureen's clothes.

"Well," Danni repeated. "I guess I'd better get my own unpacking done."

She half expected Maureen to beg her not to go, but Maureen didn't. She just nodded, her eyes on the neat stack of brown socks she had in her hands.

"Okay, well . . . see ya."

Maureen nodded again, and Danni walked through the bathroom back to room 2B. Pulling open the closet door, she thoughtfully studied some of the clothes she'd already hung up. All brand new, especially for college, and all *very* nice. She thought of Maureen's dour wardrobe and felt a guilty satisfaction at the exact rightness of her own. Which didn't necessarily mean she couldn't use some more clothes . . . there had to be a mall in Twin Falls somewhere. And she'd noticed some interesting stores along Pennsylvania Avenue on the way in.

She checked her watch. No time for mall-scoping, but plenty of time before dinner to grab a shower and change into some of her new clothes before going in search of the Commons and the Student Center.

Alone. She resolved to slip out quietly so she wouldn't get stuck with Maureen. It was one thing to be nice to Maureen, Danni decided, but she wasn't going to spend her entire first day of college with some scared rabbit of a student from who knew where. Plenty of time for dealing with Maureen later. Besides, Maureen wasn't really her roommate, right? Just her *suite*mate.

Roommates. Danni frowned, thinking of how carefully she'd filled out the roommate information form. It had been kind of a pain, but it was Salem University's policy to avoid putting the first-year students in singles.

Of course, she could probably have gotten around it. There was off-campus housing — she remembered seeing a creepy-looking brick house on the way in, with a sign by the driveway that said *Nightingale Hall, Salem University*.

But that place had looked pretty scary — not a place you'd want to visit, much less live in. And anyway, living in a dorm like that wasn't the same as being on campus, with everyone else around. People thought being rich was wonderful, but Danni knew better. How would they like to be raised by nannies and nurses and housekeepers, constantly hedged in, overprotected, and watched?

Danni made a face. Being in an all-girl dorm with a housemother and visiting hours for guys was apparently pretty overprotected, too. But how was she supposed to know it was uncool to live in a dorm like that?

Well, in spite of it all, Danni was looking forward to life in the dorm, to people and noise and laughter. To having a roommate. Someone to talk to. Someone to trust with confidences.

She just hoped her roommate was someone she'd like. . . .

Suppose she was someone like Maureen?

Or even Lacey? Danni could see how living with someone like Lacey could be a problem.

In the next room, she could hear Maureen moving haltingly about, putting her things away. And what was that sound?

Oh, no. Maureen was talking to herself, in a way that sounded definitely demented.

Maureen. Lacey. And — who? *Who* was her roommate?

And where was she?

Maybe having a roommate wasn't going to be as much fun as she'd thought.

"With my luck," muttered Danni, picking up her towel and heading for the shower, "I'll probably get the psycho roommate from hell."

Chapter 3

A half hour later, Danni slipped out the front door of room 2B while Maureen was still muttering and unpacking. The Quad, which was one of the newer, more modern buildings on campus, really was, as Kendra had said, four separate dormitories. The identical long buildings of weathered brick were set in a square with a green, landscaped courtyard in the middle. The only way in and out of the Quad was through Quad Main, the reception area on one side.

The Quad was like a fortress, Danni thought. Maybe calling the basement the Dungeon wasn't so far off the mark.

For a moment, it made her feel creepy. Closed in. Claustrophobic.

But as she walked through Quad Main, where an R.A. was on duty behind the reception desk, her common sense reasserted itself. It wasn't like she couldn't leave when she wanted to. And there were other dorms with cooler rules, if it really got to her.

Smiling a little, she pushed open one of the huge, heavy carved oak entrance doors of Quad Main and walked out into the late afternoon sun. The air was still warm, but with the faint scent of autumn. The first leaves had fallen, and swirled gracefully on the manicured lawns of the various buildings she passed: Griswold Hall, a science lab visible through its lower windows; Briggs Dormitory; Colette House, a dormitory for French majors, where only French could be spoken. Like the dorm she'd seen earlier, Nightingale Hall, each building was marked with a sign that gave its name and the name of the university.

People moved briskly, carrying boxes and suitcases and trunks in and out of the dorms, consulting maps and staring up at buildings. Freshmen, thought Danni, and then realized, I'm one, too. Upperclassmen were shouting instructions and cheerful abuse at one another, greeting people they hadn't seen all summer. At the edge of Salem Commons, she stopped.

"Wow," she said, softly.

"Yeah, that grass needs cutting bad, doesn't it?" said a voice behind her.

Danni turned. "Just what I was thinking," she said.

She hadn't been, of course. What she'd been thinking was how spectacular it looked, the broad expanse of velvet lawn, the stately oaks and ancient evergreens, the mullioned windows peering down from venerable weathered buildings covered in ivy. Like something in a book, she'd been thinking, with a rush of delicious pleasure at being part of it all.

But she wasn't about to admit that to the guy she'd turned to find standing beside her. If she'd thought the view was spectacular before, she was even more impressed with it now. He was the sort of guy who definitely improved the scenery.

"Want to wade across the grass with me?" he asked.

"Why not?" She fell into step beside him, glad she hadn't listened to the promptings of her better self and waited for Maureen.

"You're a freshman, right?" he asked, smiling easily into her eyes. He was just her height, not very tall for a guy, but, she noted in a quick glance, with a great bod.

He caught the glance and smiled more broadly. She felt color begin to warm her cheeks and said quickly, "Yes, I am. I'm not going to ask how you can tell."

"Because I don't remember Salem looking this good last year. Which means you're either a freshman or a transfer student. . . ."

It was a neatly done compliment, and an uncanny echo of her own thoughts. She couldn't help smiling back at him as he led the way up the wide, shallow flagstone steps onto the terrace that ran across one side of the dining hall.

"You made a wise decision," he told her. "Eat here early in the year, while the food is still fresh. After that, you're on your own."

She made a face and laughed, and he kept her laughing all the way through the cafeteria line. When they'd gotten through it, he led the way to a table near the door. "I myself," he confided as they sat down, "am learning to cook."

"Jordan's next line is to ask you to dinner," said a soft southern-accented voice from behind Danni. "Be careful. He claims to be learning to cook, but those of us who have eaten his food know better."

A large, muscular guy sporting a ponytail

and a pair of wire-rim glasses slid in next to Danni. "Hello," he said. "I'm Travis."

"Danni," she said.

"Jordan," said Jordan. "Travis, go away."

"Nah," said Travis. He said confidentially to Danni, "He's my roommate, can you believe it?"

"Housemate," corrected Jordan. "We live in the Kennels."

"The Kennels? I've heard there's a dungeon under the Quad, but — "

"Whoa!" Travis shook his head. "Have you been in the Dungeon? Because we've heard rumors." He lowered his voice. "What do you women do down there? They say no man has ever seen the Dungeon . . . and lived. . . ."

"I haven't seen it, either," Danni said, shaking her head. "But we've got a meeting there tonight. I'll keep my eyes open for skeletons in chains. How did you guys end up in a place called the Kennels?"

"Kennelham Hall," Jordan explained. "A small alternative residence for those whose lifestyle is not suited to the larger collective environment."

"We got kicked out of the regular dorms," Travis said. "A slight misunderstanding over the rules of partying."

"So they gave you your own dorm?"

"It's a plot," Jordan said mournfully. "They figure we'll party till we drop dead, and then they'll be rid of us."

"It could work," Travis said. "Definitely it could work."

By the time Danni had finished dinner and walked back to the Quad with Travis and Jordan, she'd agreed to come to a party that weekend at the Kennels. "Bring a friend," Travis urged, peering through his glasses at the girls streaming in and out of Quad Main. "Bring *several* friends."

Danni thought of Maureen and Lacey. And of her unknown roommate. "I'll do my best," she promised and, borrowing a gesture from Lacey, waved over her shoulder as she pushed through the door. "See ya," she called, without turning back.

To Danni's surprise, Lacey had returned to the suite. Sticking her head through the open door of room 2A, Danni observed that the chaos had retreated a little, and now was mostly confined to Lacey's side of the room.

"I thought you had a hot date," Danni said.

"A *short* hot date," Lacey shot back. "I didn't

want to get tied down on my first day on campus."

"The dorm meeting is in ten minutes," volunteered Maureen, who was sitting on the bed, her back pressed against the headboard, her arms wrapped around her drawn-up knees. It looked like a sort of upright fetal position, Danni thought.

"Well, let's go check out the action," cried Lacey instantly.

"It's in the Dungeon," Maureen said.

"The Dungeon? Whips? Chains? This school is *definitely* my kind of place."

"The *basement*, Lacey," said Danni. "That's what the basement of the Quad's called. Come on."

"Wow," breathed Lacey as they made their way through the halls and down one flight of stairs after another. "You weren't kidding! This really is a dungeon."

"Ten times around it is half a mile," a thin girl in bicycle shorts and a bulky sweater next to them volunteered as they pushed open the door at the bottom of the stairs.

"I'll keep that in mind," muttered Lacey.

"Look," said Maureen, with the first real note of enthusiasm Danni had heard from her yet. "The laundry rooms!" She darted away from them to peer into one of the rooms opening off the seemingly endless hall. Danni's eyes met Lacey's and they both began to laugh.

"What's so funny?" asked Maureen, rejoining them.

Lacey shook her head and Danni said quickly, "That looks like the all-important vending machine section."

"There's a piano room, too." Maureen pointed.

"And a weight room." Even Lacey was beginning to sound a little awed. "This Dungeon is like a whole city. Like if you had to you could stay here indefinitely, you know? Maybe even forever. I mean, if you were under seige, or got trapped in an earthquake, say, or something, you'd *never* have to leave."

Danni looked at the narrow corridors of concrete block veined overhead with pipes and valves that stretched away in either direction. No windows. Low ceilings. Tubes of glaring fluorescent lights.

A sudden sense of claustrophobia swept over her. She closed her eyes and put her hand out to steady herself against the cool stone of the wall.

"Danni? You okay?" asked Maureen.

"Fine," said Danni, opening her eyes. Ahead, the girls from her dorm were walking into a large room and settling down on the chairs and sofas scattered around it. The buzz of talking echoed in the small space.

Danni looked back over her shoulder. Girls were still coming through the door at the bottom of the stairs, laughing, talking. The basement hall went on and on and on, a cave of lighted stone. She couldn't see the end.

It gave her the creeps.

She met Lacey's and Maureen's eyes. Lacey's eyes were curious, almost calculating. Maureen's were puzzled.

Neither one of them would understand the sudden premonition that had come over her. She pulled her hand away from the cold stone and brushed her hair back from her face.

"I'm fine," Danni repeated. "Let's go get a seat and be good little freshwomen and listen to all the rules and regulations." She smiled at Lacey. "After all, how can you break the rules if you don't know what they are?"

Maureen's eyes remained puzzled, but Lacey's lit up with glee.

"Oh, excellent," she crooned. "*Excellent.* I'm so glad we're all roommates."

Chapter 4

Between orientation and registration, the next couple of days passed quickly. Danni was beginning to feel a bit more comfortable with college life, except for one thing.

There was still no sign of her roommate, and for some reason, it was beginning to make her a little uneasy.

Meanwhile, life went on as usual in suite 2AB. The phone, which was inconveniently hung on the bathroom wall between the two rooms, rang constantly. Although the calls were usually for Lacey, Maureen had already received two phone calls that had made her go into the bathroom, close the doors to both rooms 2A and 2B, and talk in a low, earnest tone of voice.

"Who is he?" asked Lacey, the second time Maureen came out.

Maureen had answered, her chin going up, "My parents."

Lacey had said, "Oh," and then, unexpectedly, "so, you and Danni have something in common, right? Danni already called her parents, haven't you, Danni?"

"Very observant, Lacey. Yes, that was my parents last night," Danni admitted. What was Lacey doing — spying on her? Danni wondered.

"My parents are going to call me once a week," said Maureen.

Lacey made a prim face. But she didn't say anything, and Danni said ruefully to Maureen, "Well, I'm going to talk to mine once a week, too." Maureen had looked pleased.

The truth was, while Danni kept wondering about her mystery roommate, she found herself liking both Lacey and Maureen. Lacey's exuberance and irreverence made them all laugh, in spite of her occasionally sharp tongue. And Maureen was even beginning to lose a little of her lost, scared look.

Until Jordan called to remind Danni about the party at the Kennel that weekend.

"It's for you," Lacey said, who had managed to pick up the receiver, answer it, and still continue to study her face in the bathroom mirror as she applied makeup.

Danni got up from her desk and took the phone from Lacey's outstretched hand.

"A guy," Lacey said softly. "Not a paternal-sounding type."

"Hello," said Danni, pulling the receiver to the end of the cord and sitting down on the floor with her back against the foot of her bed.

"Hey," said a husky voice. "Remember me?"

"What?"

"*Jordan*," said the voice indignantly.

"Oh, hi, Jordan," said Danni. "Of course I remember you."

"Aha," said Lacey from the bathroom.

"Are you coming to our party?" Jordan asked.

"Absolutely, I'm coming to your party," said Danni. "Tell me all the sordid details."

"Aha!" said Lacey again, and the moment Danni hung up the phone, she said, "My favorite words: party and sordid. Tell me, tell me."

Danni went into the bathroom and leaned against the wall so both Lacey and Maureen, who was lying on her bed, reading, could hear.

"Big party this Saturday night at Kennelham Hall, also known as the Kennels. And we're all invited."

"All right! *Decent*," cried Lacey.

Maureen's eyes got enormous behind her glasses. "I can't," she almost whimpered.

"Girl, are you serious?" Lacey shoved her makeup unceremoniously back into the bathroom cabinet and pushed past Danni to stand by Maureen's bed with her hands on her hips. She regarded Maureen as if Maureen were some strange species of animal.

Danni felt a pang of sympathy and annoyance for the beleaguered girl, who had picked up her pillow and pressed it against her chest defensively. As an only child, Danni understood what it was like to feel awkward around others. But a little voice inside Danni asked, couldn't Maureen even *try*?

Sensitivity was not Lacey's strong suit. "Get real, Maureen. The first weekend on campus and we've already been invited to a major party . . ."

"It didn't sound like a particularly exclusive invitation," Danni pointed out. "Jordan said, among other things, 'Bring women. *Lots* of women. . . .'"

But Lacey shrugged it off. "It beats all the

boring orientation things the administration has set up. I mean, a freshman party at the Student Center?"

"I think they thought it would be fun for us," said Danni.

"I think they're out of their minds," returned Lacey bluntly. She focused on Maureen. "Listen, Maureen. It's *critical* to get out and be seen. This is an *excellent* opportunity."

"I can't," Maureen repeated, her voice a teary whisper.

"Good grief!" cried Lacey, throwing her arms out dramatically.

Danni gave Lacey a warning frown, then sat down on Maureen's desk chair, straddling it so she could rest her chin on her hands on the back of the chair. She asked, soothingly, "What's wrong, Maureen?"

With a gulp, Maureen said, "Me! I'm wrong. You don't understand!"

"You're shy," said Danni. "That's okay. We'll be there. You'll know us."

"No! No, you don't know what it's like! People staring at you. Expecting you to say something. And then laughing at you when you don't."

"Are you *kidding*?" asked Lacey. "Where

have you been all your life? Didn't they ever let you out?"

Maureen's eyes widened. "W-what?"

"Lacey, don't be so mean," Danni said quickly. To Maureen she said, "Listen, it'll be okay. We'll be there."

"Yeah," said Lacey, "So you don't need to get so hysterical, Maureen."

Ignoring Lacey, Danni said, "Lots of people are shy, okay, Maureen? You just have to practice. With practice, anybody can act normal!"

Lacey hooted. "Who wants to be *normal*? *Bor*-ing!"

"Lacey!" Danni said. Then turning back to Maureen she said, "What you need is some confidence in yourself."

"Yeah. C'mon, Maureen, what are you? A woman or a mouse?"

Maureen jumped. "How did you know! How did you guess my nickname?"

"Your nickname . . . ?" Although Lacey often and loudly proclaimed that she wasn't a real student, she was as quick as she was uncannily observant. "You mean *mouse*? *Mouse* is your nickname?"

Danni gave an inward groan as Maureen nodded, the dull color flooding her face. Didn't

Maureen know Lacey well enough by now to know that Lacey would grab on to the embarrassing nickname for all it was worth? Maureen was doomed to be called Mouse from now on, not just by Lacey, but, by the time Lacey was through, by all of Salem U. And how could Maureen, who all too clearly resembled her nickname, ever live it down?

Sure enough, "I like it!" Lacey cried, her eyes glowing. "Mouse! We have a mouse around the house!"

"Lacey," admonished Danni.

"It's okay," said Maureen unexpectedly. Although she was still blushing, she was smiling a little, too. "It makes me feel less . . . homesick. Everyone in my family calls me that, you know."

"See, Danni?" said Lacey. "Besides, it's not *my* fault Mouse is Maureen's nickname."

"Really, I'd rather be called Mouse," said Maureen. "I really and truly would."

"Are you sure?" asked Danni.

"Why not?" asked Maureen.

What could Danni say to that? As Lacey grinned impishly, Danni gave in. "Okay. Mouse."

But she shook her head. Much as she liked

Lacey, Danni was, for the moment, glad she wasn't sharing a room with her.

She was beginning to really wonder about her absent roommate, though. Who knew what she'd be like when she showed up. What kind of roommate had to come late? It was weird.

"Speaking of names," she said aloud, keeping her thoughts to herself, "I found out my roomie's name from Kendra. It's Margot. And she'll be here today or tomorrow."

As if she could read Danni's mind, Lacey said, "How come so late? Pretty weird."

Danni shrugged, but a sense of uneasiness persisted. If Lacey thought something was weird, it probably was pretty weird. "Kendra said that's all she knew. That my roomie had chosen not to participate in the orientation programs."

"Maybe she's trying to make a grand entrance," said Lacey. Then she lowered her voice and added ominously, "Or maybe they wouldn't let her out of the looney bin until the last minute. . . ."

Before either Mouse or Danni could answer, a perfunctory knock sounded on the door, which was almost immediately thrust open. A short, muscular girl with tightly curled damp hair and the top of a tank suit showing through her partially unzipped Salem U. sweatshirt stuck her head in the door. Her dark skin was damp, as if she'd just gotten out of the shower or the swimming pool.

"Caren just got the first care package from home," she announced.

Lacey wrinkled her nose. "Euuw, Jodie — You smell like chlorine."

"What do you expect?" asked Jodie Johnson, unperturbed. "I just got back from swim practice."

"Anything good in the package?" asked Danni.

"Dunno," answered Jodie, leaving. "But you'd better hurry. I'm hungry enough to eat anything. Coach worked us to death today."

"Then we'd better hurry," said Lacey, charging after Jodie. "Wow, can you believe it? We haven't even been here a week and already someone's getting care packages from home. Kinda makes you feel like you never escaped. . . ."

"Oh my God," cried Caren Sanchez as the three roommates followed Jodie Johnson into the room next door. "It's a flock of vultures."

"The food in the care package is that bad?" asked Lacey.

Jodie had seized the box and was sorting through the contents. "Not unless you don't like chocolate-chip macadamia-nut cookies," she announced. "And blondies. *And* brownies. And look at this! A box of chocolates. And . . . what's this?"

Jodie held up a large round loaf of bread and Caren burst out laughing. "Sourdough bread. Don't forget, I'm from San Francisco. Those chocolates are See's chocolates. They're my favorites. They come from there, too!"

"Outstanding," said Lacey. "A food orgy. Let's get started."

Jodie handed around the care package and the five of them settled down for an evening of food and gossip. As they laughed and talked, Danni studied the pairs of roommates. Athletic Jodie Johnson and studious Caren Sanchez were very different. But they seemed to get along fine. And for that matter, so did Lacey and Maureen, more or less. Didn't they?

But she was still uneasy. Who was this Margot? What made her so late? Did she have something to hide? What could it be. . . .

Stop it, Danni, she told herself. She's probably just getting back from a family vacation or something. That was it. Not to worry. She would probably like her roommate just fine —

"Suicide."

The hush-voiced whisper of the word caught Danni's attention. "What did you say, Jodie?"

"At Nightingale Hall," said Jodie. "One of the off-campus dorms. Only they're calling it *Nightmare* Hall, now."

"What happened?" demanded Lacey with ghoulish glee.

"A girl named Giselle committed suicide there last spring. The housemother found her." Jodie lowered her voice. "She'd hung herself in her room."

Maureen's face had gotten paper-white. She whispered, "Does anyone have to live in her room this year?"

"Sure," said Jodie. "Can you imagine — your roommate is a ghost!"

"Jodie, that is gross," Caren told her roommate firmly. "Where do you hear all this stuff, anyway?"

"On the swim team. One of the swimmers, Linda Carlyle, is living in Nightmare Hall. Not in Giselle's actual room, though. At least, I don't think so."

Lacey and Caren made ghoulish faces and snickered.

Maureen didn't. She shook her head reproachfully.

And Danni only forced a smile. It seemed wrong, somehow, to gossip about a girl who had died so unhappily. Wrong to laugh while talking about it.

Poor girl, she thought. How awful. And how sad.

Danni's last thoughts as she fell asleep late that night were about the girl who had died.

No matter how bad things got, Danni thought, I'd fight to stay alive. I'd fight . . . to the death, I'd fight . . .

The dream was familiar somehow. She was alone. It was very dark. She groped through stifling blackness, trying to find a light. But all she found was darkness.

Darkness and the sound of her own breathing. Harder and harder. Harder and harder as she groped more and more frantically through the dark.

Then she heard it.

Breathing.

Breathing in the darkness just ahead.

She wasn't alone.

It was waiting.

It could see her.

But she couldn't see it.

Trying to scream, Danni woke up.

She was safe. Safe in her own room. In her own bed.

It was only a dream.

Only a nightmare.

Then she heard it.

Breathing.

She wasn't alone.

Chapter 5

"Hello," said a cool voice, and a light came on.

Blinded, Danni scrambled up to her knees on her bed, clutching the sheets.

A dark figure filled the doorway. It didn't move.

"You-who-who are you?" gasped Danni.

For a moment, the figure didn't answer. Then it glided forward into the room like a ghost.

"Who — Gi-Giselle?" gasped Danni, blinking, trying to adjust her eyes to the sudden flood of light.

"You sound like an owl," the figure said. "Who's Giselle? I'm Margot. Margot Hanes. You must be my roommate."

Still gripped by her nightmare, Danni just stared. *This* was her new roommate? In the middle of the night?

"How-how did you get in?" Nervously, Danni grasped the sheet and pulled it higher around her.

"Through Quad Main, how else? And of course, I have a key to the room. But the door wasn't locked. Do you always sleep with your door unlocked?"

"No. Yes. I don't know." Danni took a deep breath. Had she locked the door? Of course she had. Checking to see if a door was locked was a habit of long standing, something she did almost as automatically as breathing.

But maybe she hadn't. After all, why would Margot Hanes lie about something like that?

Shake it off, Danni, she told herself. Don't act like such a wimp.

She straightened her shoulders, reached up to push her hair back, and smiled. "I'm Danni Spelling." She paused, but her new roommate didn't say anything, so Danni went on. "I guess you startled me a little. I didn't know when to expect you."

The girl looked blankly at Danni. "No. Why should you?"

How did she do that? Danni wondered. How did she ask questions that made you feel gauche and stupid?

Margot set a rolled-up quilt and pillow down on her bare mattress. Then she opened her suitcase and carried some things into the bathroom, returning a few minutes later. She was not tall, Danni saw, as the nightmare moment of waking up from her dream had made Margot seem, just medium. She had soft medium brown hair almost as long as Danni's, but parted on one side and hanging straight to her collarbone. The summer seemed to have left her with the remnants of a tan as well as a faint dusting of freckles across her nose. Her eyes looked dark and intense in the half-lit room, but all in all, she looked practically wholesome. Just the sort of roommate parents would want for their daughters. A good girl.

Danni tried to watch Margot without staring as she pulled a long, white bathrobe from her suitcase. Her new roommate. Her nice, average, yet oddly mysterious new roommate.

"Where are you going?" asked Danni.

"To take a shower," said the girl, as if it were the most logical thing in the world to take a shower so late at night. "Don't let me keep you from your sleep."

"Oh, no, don't worry," said Danni. "I mean, I'm awake, now."

"I'm sorry," said Margot, and glided out of the room, closing the door firmly behind her.

Is this how Mouse feels? wondered Danni. Always at a loss for words?

Danni resolved to stay awake until Margot returned. The late minutes ticked by. The dorm wasn't quiet, exactly. It was never quiet. But all the sounds had slowed and muffled, as most of the people in the dorm were sleeping. Danni tilted her head, her eyes narrowed in concentration. Was that the sound of the shower she heard? No, it wasn't possible. She was just imagining it. The showers were too far away for her to hear anything.

Odd of Margot to arrive so late at night. Where had she come from? Where were the rest of her things?

Danni looked around. A black, bulky-looking shoulder bag had been dropped on the desk chair. I could look in there, she thought. Find out something about her.

But the thought made Danni cringe. What if Margot found Danni looking through her purse? What an invasion of privacy! Margot would think she had a snoop for a roommate. Or worse, what if she thought Danni was a thief?

The thought was mortifying.

Chill out, Danni thought. It's late. She's tired, you're tired. You can start getting to know each other in the morning.

A door slammed in the distance. Creepy, Danni's thoughts went on disjointedly. Creepy to be taking a shower in the middle of the night. Creepy to be in the long, mirror-shiny room, with the echoing tiles and the high, tiny, opaque windows. There was a door at each end, though. It wasn't like you could be trapped . . .

What was Margot *doing* in the shower? Maybe I don't want to know, thought Danni.

It was all wrong. It wasn't supposed to be like this.

Margot still hadn't come back. Danni could feel herself falling asleep, was helpless to stop herself. It was like falling over a cliff, falling . . .

For a moment, on the edge between sleeping and waking, between the light and the dark, she thought she heard a sound. For a moment, she thought Margot had come back into the room, had glided soundlessly across the floor to stand above Danni's bed and stare down at her.

But when she forced her leaden eyelids apart for a second, the room was empty and cold. Danni pulled the covers up.

No law, she thought drowsily. No law says I have to like my roommate.

Still, it'll be too bad if she's not going to be my friend.

Too bad, she thought. But before she could think what was too bad, she fell into a deep and dreamless sleep.

Margot slipped quietly back into the room, wrapping the institutional plain-white robe around her.

Good. Her roommate was asleep. Margot stood motionless for a long moment, listening to Danni's even breathing. Then she glided to the foot of Danni's bed and stood staring down at her.

Her eyes took in the jumble of shiny, expensive new cosmetics on top of the chest of drawers, the tangle of jewelry that had the gleam of what could only be real gold. She reached out and ran her finger delicately, carefully, down the sweater that had been draped carelessly across the foot of the bed.

Cashmere, of course. It gave her a little shiver of delight.

And envy.

Danni sighed and turned over.

Quickly Margot backed away. She threw a sheet and her quilt over the bed — she'd make it up more carefully the next day. With measured haste, she hung the bathrobe on the back of the bathroom door and slid into the narrow dormitory bed, drawing her knees up under her chin and wrapping her arms around them. She looked around the Spartan dorm room with satisfaction. This was it. She'd arrived at last. It had been a long, hard trip, taking every ounce of intelligence and strength and stubbornness, and yes, cunning, to get here. But she'd beaten the seemingly impossible odds. And it would be worth it. She'd make sure of that.

It was so quiet. She savored the late night peacefulness. She'd worried about living in a dorm at first. Worried about being with all those people. She'd had enough of roommates and people and horrible cheerful insane friendliness. Insane . . .

No, no. She stopped herself. She had to stop thinking that way. There was nothing crazy about ambition. What was crazy was the way people tried to stop you, hold you back. Even the well-meaning ones.

Sometimes they were the worst.

But now she had to forget all that. This was her chance to start fresh. To be the person she wanted to be.

She had earned it. She deserved it.

Turning her head, she studied the sleeping form across the room from her from a safer distance. Danni Spelling. The honey-gold of her hair was spread out across the pillow. Her head was sideways on the pillow, revealing a pure, almost angelic profile. Long dark lashes lay against the smooth, pale cheeks.

Margot thought again of how painstakingly, how carefully she'd filled out her roommate form. It was very important to get the right roommate. Just the right roommate.

But was this the one?

I wonder, thought Margot. Could this one be trusted? Could she handle the truth? Or would she be like all the others. . . ?

She didn't look like the others. She looked just right. Although she didn't look like someone who could understand what Margot had been through. How could someone that pale and perfect and golden understand what Margot's life had been like?

For a moment, Margot felt a flash of resentment, but she quickly brought it under control. Someone like Danni could teach her a lot. And she had a lot to learn.

Be grateful, she told herself. Be grateful for what you've got.

The perfect roommate.

Yes. Oh, yes.

Danni sat up slowly the next morning. She had had such a long, strange dream. Not quite a nightmare, but . . . She yawned and stretched. Nightmare Hall. It had been all that talk of Nightmare Hall and ghostly roommates. There were no such things as ghosts. Or haunted houses. Or haunted dormitories, for that matter.

Or were there? Danni looked around and rubbed her eyes. And realized that it hadn't been a dream at all. An alien presence *had* invaded 2B after all.

But where was she? Where was Margot? The long, white bathrobe on the back of the bathroom door caught Danni's eye. Wherever Margot was, she must have gotten dressed and gone out.

Almost without thinking, Danni slipped out of bed. In another moment she was standing by her roommate's bed.

How neatly it was made. All tightly tucked with hospital corners and the worn quilt and sheets pulled up and folded over just so. Noticing that one of the drawers of the chest of drawers was not quite shut, Danni impulsively pulled it open.

Her eyes widened. Except for several stacks of serviceable underwear, four neatly rolled pairs of socks, and a pair of very faded jeans it was almost empty.

Quickly she pulled the next drawer open, and the next. Empty.

Shutting the bottom drawer she straightened to meet her own face in the mirror above the dresser. Her hand crept up to her cheek. How could she have done that? What would Margot do if she caught her? It was as if someone else had taken control of Danni.

She couldn't bear to meet her own eyes in the mirror. She looked down.

And froze.

How could she not have seen it before? It was the only thing on top of the chest of drawers, the same sharp silver as the mirror.

But more deadly.

Danni licked her lips. Reached out to touch it.

But she couldn't.
Something warned her not to.
She closed her eyes. Opened them again.
It was still there.
A knife.

Chapter 6

How long had she been standing there? It seemed forever. She didn't remember picking up the knife. But she must have. The sound of it clattering down onto the scarred wood top of the chest of drawers brought her to her senses.

Trembling, she reached out to still the noise.

"What are you doing?"

Danni jumped like a guilty child. "Oh! You scared me!"

Margot's voice was not like she remembered it — not cool and distant. Now it was harsh, threatening as she advanced with measured menace toward Danni.

"I said, what are you doing? Have you been going through my things?"

Backing away, Danni shook her head mutely.

"Answer me," said Margot harshly. "Have you been going through my things?"

"No! No, I — I . . ." Danni looked wildly around.

Margot picked up the knife. "I saw you with this in your hand. It's mine. Don't touch anything of mine unless you ask."

"Of course! I wouldn't!"

Margot held up the knife, staring at it. Then she laid it carefully back down on the dresser. The rage seemed to drain out of her. She looked at Danni and said, softly, "Okay. I trust you."

"Hey, what's happening?" Lacey shoved the bathroom door open and stuck her head in. Both Danni and Margot jumped.

"Lacey, don't you ever knock?" said Danni, clenching her still shaking hands into fists.

Lacey didn't seem to notice. She was studying Margot, a puzzled expression on her face. Then she grinned. "The mystery roommate. Right?"

Margot nodded.

Undeterred by Margot's lack of response, Lacey said, "So when did you get here?"

"Late last night. My trip was delayed."

"Flight delay, huh? Don't you *hate* hanging around airports? Course it's better than bus stations."

"You hang around bus stations?" asked Margot, her face serious.

Lacey burst out laughing. "Sure. That was good, Margot!"

Margot said, "How did you know my name?"

"A little paranoid, aren't you? Kendra, the R.A., told Danni and Danni told me. I'm Lacey. I live through that wannabe bathroom in room 2A. We're suitemates."

"Oh," said Margot.

Lacey looked over at the top of Margot's chest of drawers. "Hey, nice letter opener."

"Letter opener?" croaked Danni.

"Big family? A ton of friends? Heavy mail expectations?" queried Lacey. "Letters," she lowered her voice, "from a guy?"

"It's very old. A family . . . heirloom."

Lacey lost interest in the letter opener. "You got here just in time, Margot, didn't she, Danni? We were beginning to wonder about you."

Danni didn't think it was possible for Margot to look more tense, but she suddenly did. "What do you mean?"

Instead of answering, Lacey asked, "Do you like to party? *That* is the question."

Margot hesitated. Then she said, "Who doesn't?"

"Good. Because we have a party lined up tonight." Lacey yawned hugely. "Your new roomie will tell you all about it. I've *got* to take a nap."

"Lacey, you just got up," said Danni. Her hands had stopped shaking. She was feeling more normal. In fact, she was feeling sort of silly. She'd been making way too big a deal out of everything.

"Consistency is the hobgoblin of little minds," answered Lacey airily, and disappeared back through the bathroom.

"Huh?" said Danni.

"I think she's quoting Ben Franklin or Ralph Waldo Emerson," said Margot.

"Huh?" repeated Danni again, staring at Margot. "Are you kidding? Lacey doesn't even know who those guys are."

"I expect she had to, to get into Salem University," said Margot. "Salem does have fairly high academic standards."

Danni laughed. "Nah, not Lacey. Her family's all alums, and they've made a few major donations to Salem, too."

"Is that what Lacey said?" asked Margot. Danni was surprised by the faint frown that creased her forehead. What was bothering Margot?

Again she felt that faint sense of unease, too vague to really put a finger on. It was like one of those children's games: What's wrong with this picture?

But before Danni could figure it out, Margot shrugged. "Never mind. What about this party tonight? I haven't got anything to wear. My-my stuff — the rest of it — hasn't gotten here yet."

She looked hard at Danni, as if daring her in some way.

Or as if, thought Danni, she knew I'd looked at her stuff. She suddenly wondered how long Margot had been standing in the doorway, watching, before she'd spoken. How long?

The thought gave Danni the creeps. And made her feel ashamed. What if Margot *had* seen her going through her drawers?

Almost against her will, as if she were compelled to make it up to Margot, Danni said, "Hey, no prob. I've got all kinds of things. We're about the same size. You can have anything you need. After all, that's what roommates are for, right?"

Margo hesitated. Then she smiled, a tentative, experimental smile, as if she wasn't used to smiling.

As if, thought Danni, she'd learned how to smile from a book, and practiced it in mirrors.

"Right?" prompted Danni again.

"Right," echoed Margot at last. "That's what roommates are for."

Chapter 7

The four roommates walked across campus. From the sounds coming from the dormitories and sororities and fraternities, it seemed the whole campus had decided to party on the first Saturday night of the semester.

But while it seemed like fun and music and laughter were everywhere, Danni's mind returned to the story she'd heard the other day, about the girl who'd died in Nightingale Hall — *Nightmare* Hall. She couldn't help wondering if something sinister lurked in any of these other dorms.

Lacey was having no such worries. "Serious!" she cried happily as a blast of music and raucous cheering seemed to shake the foundations of one of the frat houses they were passing.

Mouse gave an inarticulate squeak and shrank back. "It's so *loud*!"

Lacey laughed with manic glee. "C'mon," she said. "We're wasting time!"

Mouse turned to Margot. "I've never been to a party like this," she said. "Have you?"

"Don't worry," Margot told her. "Just act like you know what you're doing, and no one will know."

Mouse nodded obediently, and Danni felt a flash of amusement. It was as if Mouse had adopted Margot as some kind of security blanket, even though they had only met a few hours before. Margot had managed to fix Mouse's glasses so at least they weren't held together with a paper clip. And if Mouse didn't look spectacular, she did look passable, thought Danni, surveying Mouse's jeans and oxford shirt and sweater. The shirt was, unfortunately, buttoned all the way to the throat, but who knew? Maybe normal people at Salem dressed that way sometimes.

Right, thought Danni.

The rest of them looked a little more outstanding, at least: Lacey in what had to be the world's shortest skirt, with a soft, *seemingly* demure cashmere sweater over it. Her over-the-knee boots made the skirt look even shorter — or maybe they just made the long expanse of Lacey's thighs even more noticeable. Danni had opted for a cropped lambswool sweater over her best jeans. She looked, she decided, good, but not *too* good. Margot was wearing a pair of black jeans and had, reluctantly, allowed Danni to talk her into borrowing one of Danni's sweaters, of amber cashmere. The color brought out the tawniness of Margot's hair and complexion. Her eyes were a deep and unsettling green. Even the rich amber color didn't warm them.

"Where is this place, anyway?" Mouse said apprehensively.

"We're almost there. Jordan said it was just across Pennsylvania Avenue, near the north corner of the campus," Danni explained. "He said we couldn't miss it . . ." Her voice trailed off.

The four of them stopped on the sidewalk. They'd reached Kennelham Hall. All they could do was stare in shock.

Then Lacey choked out, "He wasn't kidding about not being able to m-m-miss it," and started to laugh. Beside her, Margot joined in.

Mouse's voice went up into the glass-shattering range: "We're going in *there?*"

Kennelham Hall was made of red brick draped in traditional ivy, like many of the older buildings at Salem. But if it was traditional in structure, it was anything but traditional in decoration. A giant stuffed dog with an extra-long tongue of red felt was tied above the porch, a party hat askew on its head. Beneath it was an elaborate banner that proclaimed *The Kennels.* Every window in the house was flung open, as if the roar of the music had blasted through them. Strings of lights festooned the ivy, the dog, the windows, and every tree and bush around the house.

"God," gasped Lacey, trying to regain her composure. "It looks like an escapee from the tacky Christmas decoration hall of fame. Have you ever seen *anything* like it?"

"No," said Danni truthfully. "It is definitely . . ."

"Unique," supplied Margot.

"I don't like this," moaned Mouse.

"What's not to like?" answered Lacey, able to stop laughing at last. "Come on."

"But what if it's a *really* wild party? What if it gets out of control? What if the police come?" cried Mouse.

"What if we leave you standing here on the street?" Lacey shot back. Leading the way, she plunged up the front steps of the Kennels.

Mouse's voice trailed off. She stood uncertainly on the front walk for a moment as her three roommates headed into the party. A figure reeled out from the bushes.

"Hello, hello!" he shouted genially. "C'mon in to our lil' partyyyy!"

Mouse gave the cheerfully loud boy a frightened look, squeaked once, incoherently, and fled up the stairs after her roommates.

The bell tolled, long, slow mournful strokes. Lacey looked up from the sofa to one of her roommates standing over her. "Danni!"

"Yeah," said Danni. "Listen, Lacey, Jordan and I are headed back."

"Ask not for whom the bell tolls . . . Where's everybody?" asked Lacey, slurring her words a little. She took a sedate sip from the nearly empty cup she was holding and hiccupped. "Like Mousie? We have a mouse in our dorm room," she confided to the world at large. "I'm 'fraid of those little mousies, aren't you?"

"Get a cat," suggested the boy sitting next to her, looking amused.

"Danni looks like a cat, don't you, Danni? That's Danni. She's another one of my roommates. *She's* not a mouse."

Was Lacey as out of it as she sounded? Danni looked at her uneasily. She seemed, if anything, even more unpredictable. As if reading Danni's thoughts, Lacey looked up. Her eyes glinted in the uncertain light.

"Lacey?" said Danni.

"Party's over," said Lacey, motioning toward the room. It was true. A few people sat in groups talking quietly or sprawled on couches around the room. The music had stopped and the guy who was looking through the CDs didn't seem to be making any quick decisions. Paper cups and bottles were scattered everywhere.

"Where is Mouse?" said Lacey, the gleam appearing again in her eyes. "Did she creep out of here? And what about the mysterious Margot? Mysterious Ms. Margot. Where is she? Hmm, Danni?"

"How should I know, Lacey?"

Seeing Danni's irritation, Lacey smiled, then said abruptly, "Time to go. I'm *hungry*. Where can we get something to eat around this town?"

The boy next to her jumped up and reached

down to pull her up beside him. "Well, Twin Falls isn't New York City," the boy began.

"Pete's from New York," Lacey told Danni. "I *like* New York."

"But we'll find something that's open all night," Pete promised.

"Great," said Lacey. She addressed Danni and Jordan. "You come, too." She lowered her voice. "That's from Robert Frost."

"I don't know, Lacey," said Danni. "I kinda feel like heading home." How could she explain that she felt uneasy? That she couldn't help wondering where her new roommate was? Was she back in their room? Why had she left the party without telling anyone?

But Margot was a grown-up. She didn't owe Danni or any of them any explanations. And maybe she'd just left with some guy.

"Danni," said Lacey with exaggerated patience, interrupting Danni's thoughts. "You don't want me driving away in the middle of the night with some strange man, do you?"

Jordan nodded wisely. "She's right, Danni. Pete's from New York and he lives in the Kennels. He's definitely strange."

"But it's so late," said Danni. "Way late."

"Okay, okay." Lacey shrugged. "Up," she

said to Pete and he got up and caught Lacey's hand and pulled her to her feet. " 'Bye, boring people," said Lacey as she and Pete sauntered out the back of the house, heading for the Kennels parking lot.

Jordan looked down at Danni. Their eyes locked for a long, long moment.

"Don't," whispered Danni, looking away.

"Don't what?" whispered Jordan back. He touched her cheek. "Don't look at you? Why not? What are you afraid I'll see?"

His voice was teasing, but when she glanced back up at him through your eyelashes, she saw his face was serious. For a moment, he didn't look like the laughing, joking guy she'd been with all night. A series of quick images flashed before her eyes: Jordan dancing, spinning her gleefully around until she was dizzy and laughing, too. Jordan and Travis cutting up, pretending they were about to square off over who was going to dance with her next. Jordan. Jordan presiding over the slide-down-the-banister contest.

This wasn't the same Jordan she thought she was beginning to know. This Jordan looked completely different. So — scary serious.

"Maybe I am," Danni answered softly at last.

Jordan's voice suddenly sounded as serious as the expression on his face. "Trust me," he said. He reached out for her.

I'm going to like this, thought Danni as their lips touched. And she was right.

She did.

Until the screams began.

Chapter 8

"No, no, nooooo! Help meee!"

Danni froze in Jordan's arms. But he didn't seem to notice that or the horrible screams. He kept kissing her, kissing her, his arms tightening and tightening. . . .

"Let me go!" cried Danni. "Jordan, let me go!"

Savagely, Danni twisted free of Jordan's arms to run down the hall toward the back door and the awful shrieking. She scarcely heard Jordan's heavy footsteps pounding behind her.

Who was screaming? What had happened? Was Kennelham a nightmare dorm, too?

Her heart racing, Danni burst out the door. She stopped dead.

"Lacey!" Danni couldn't believe her eyes.

Leaning against Pete, Lacey was laughing

uncontrollably. "Oh, oh, oh," gasped Lacey. "You should see your faces!"

Pete grinned broadly. "She's crazy," he said, his arm around Lacey's shoulders.

"Somebody is!" exclaimed Jordan. "What-d'ya let her scare us like that for?"

Pete shrugged.

"I really had you going, didn't I?" said Lacey.

Danni had always had a quick temper. Now it flared up. "Lacey, have you ever heard of the girl who cried wolf? You are a jerk, you know that? You, you. . . ." Danni sputtered.

"Chill, Danni. It was *just* a joke. Besides, I *told* you guys you should come with us. I don't like it when people don't do what I want." A slow, eerie smile spread over Lacey's face. Then she lurched to one side and almost fell down.

"You're drunk," said Danni, disgustedly.

"Maybe . . . are you guys coming, or what?"

Danni and Jordan exchanged helpless glances.

"She always this wild and crazy?" asked Jordan.

"Don't ask me," Danni said.

"You should know! You're her roommate."

"For not even a week, yet, Jordan, okay?"

Danni put her hands on her hips and glared at Lacey.

"*C'mon*, Danni," said Lacey.

"Are you sober enough to drive?" Jordan asked Pete suspiciously.

"Of course!" Pete looked angry. "I don't drive drunk! What do you think I am?"

Jordan raised his hands. "Sorry, okay?"

"Okay. So, are you guys coming, or what?"

The rage had deserted Danni as suddenly as it had come. "Okay, okay," she said. Putting her arm through Jordan's, she allowed herself to be led to Pete's car in the parking lot. "Don't scare me like that again, Lacey, do you hear?"

"Oh, I won't scare you like *that* again," Lacey promised. The glint that had shown in her eyes earlier appeared again. Danni was startled. It was as if someone else was looking out at Danni from behind Lacey's eyes.

Lacey stared at Danni hypnotically. Then she lowered her eyes, watching Danni slyly from beneath her lashes. "I'll think of something new."

Lacey leaned over the toilet. "Kill me now," she moaned.

"What's wrong?" asked Mouse anxiously, standing in the door of the bathroom clutching her bathrobe around her. "Are you sick?"

"I'm dying," moaned Lacey. "Kill me now. Put me out of my misery."

"You'll live," said Margot coolly from the other door.

"Are you a doctor?" said Lacey with feeble sarcasm.

"If you hadn't been so stupid about drinking, you wouldn't be driving that porcelain Cadillac," Margot answered.

Danni, who'd come up behind Margot, stifled a laugh. Her roommate was a little strange, maybe, but she was definitely cool. It took nerve to stand up to someone like Lacey. Nerve, too, to be so coldly honest.

At the moment, however, it was apparent that Lacey didn't agree.

"Thanks for the help," snapped Lacey. She pulled herself shakily to her feet and, with as much dignity as she could muster, staggered back to her room and collapsed on her bed. Her three roommates gathered in the bathroom door to stare at her, sprawled out in her nightshirt, a slipper hanging off one foot.

"Poor Lacey," said Mouse, sympathetically.

Margot snorted. "For what? Being stupid?"

Lacey opened one eye. "Thanks, Mouse, I owe *you* one for the sympathy, at least. As for you, Margot, what time did *you* get back?"

"Before you did," said Margot.

"Alone, I bet."

"You even got back before I did, remember, Margot?" Mouse rushed in.

Margot glanced at Mouse in surprise.

Mouse explained breathlessly, "I heard you in your room . . ."

Instead of answering Mouse, Margot said, "Lacey, this kind of behavior is bush league, okay?"

"Okay, *okay*," groaned Lacey. "Go away, okay?"

"We're going," said Danni.

As she and Margot went back to their room, Danni said softly, "You were kind of tough on Lacey." Behind them, they could hear Mouse's anxious voice: "Lacey, are you sure there's nothing I can do?" and Lacey's groans.

"It depends on how you look at it," Margot said. "I know I've just met Lacey, but I know. . . . I've known people like her. People who can't handle things like drinking, or whatever. People who lose control. . . ."

"Oh, I don't know," said Danni. "I think Lacey was just showing off. Trying to be extra wild to live up to her image, you know?

"Maybe," said Margot. "We'll see." She

paused, then added, "Not that I have anything against a little wild-'n-craziness. I just have a problem with people who won't admit there's something they can't handle. Who lose control and then keep on losing control. . . ."

Was Danni imagining things? A shadow seemed to have fallen across Margot's face. Poor Margot, thought Danni with one of the sudden intuitions that she had. I bet she's had that problem with someone close to her. Someone very close.

"Yeah," said Danni aloud. "Listen, want to go down to the Quad caf and get some coffee?"

Margot's face brightened. "Yes. Yes, I'd like that." She glanced conspiratorially over her shoulder toward room 2A. "Let's leave Florence Nightingale and her patient to enjoy themselves."

Stifling laughter, the two roommates quickly got dressed and snuck out of the room together.

The Quad caf was quiet in the early Sunday morning calm. Like the rest of the buildings on campus, it had the patina of long use, with oak trestle tables lined with oak chairs marching down either side of the oak-wainscotted room. Narrow mullioned windows looked out onto carefully tended beds of flowers and shrubs.

Danni heaped her plate with food, while Margot selected coffee and cereal and milk and fruit with a serious deliberation even Mouse would have admired. The two roommates settled down at a table in the corner near a window.

"Nice," said Margot, nodding toward the window, through which sunlight was streaming.

"Yes," said Danni. She dug in to her breakfast. She looked up to see Margot watching her, coffee cup cradled in her hands.

"What is it?" asked Danni. "Do I have something on my face or something?"

"No. I was just admiring your appetite."

Abashed, Danni looked down at her plate. Bacon, eggs, grits, hashbrowns, creamed chip beef, a cranberry muffin, and buttered toast. "Uh-oh," she said. "Maybe I did go a little bit overboard."

"I was just admiring your being able to eat so early in the morning."

"You know something? I like the caf food," Danni confessed. "I like being able to eat anything I want."

"I can see that," said Margot. She took another sip of coffee. "You know what? I like not having to eat everything on my plate.

That was an unwritten rule where I grew up."

"Yuck," said Danni. "I hate rules. Don't tell Lacey, but I kind of agree with her — they're made to be broken."

"Yeah." She smiled warmly. "It's great to get away from home, don't you think? Make your own rules . . . do whatever you want."

"Definitely. So, where are you from, Margot?"

"You ever been to the midwest?"

When Danni shook her head, Margot said, "Lucky you. It's flat and it's farms. I couldn't wait to get away."

"Kansas?"

"Nebraska," said Margot. "What about you?"

"My parents travel so much, it's hard to say. But I was born in California," said Danni.

"You've gotten to travel a lot? Lucky. I've always wanted to do that."

Danni shrugged. "It's fun. But it would've been nice to have a real home."

Some of her bitterness must have shown, for Margot's expression was sympathetic and she didn't ask any more questions. Giving herself a mental shake, Danni switched subjects. "So, what did you think of the party last night?"

"It was fun."

"I loved it," said Danni. "Although I'm not so sure about Jordan. He's the guy who invited us. You know, who met us right after we got there?"

Margot nodded.

"Well, I sort of ended up with him. He's okay, I guess."

"If he's not the one, he can still be some fun," Margot offered.

"True. What about you?"

"I'm still reading the menu," said Margot.

"If you could order a guy off the menu, any guy, who would it be?"

Margot laughed. "Don't tell anybody, but I like Cary Grant. In those old movies."

"Cary Grant?"

For a moment, Margot looked embarrassed. "I know, I know. He's ancient. And dead, for that matter. But I used to like to stay up late watching old movies when everybody else was asleep."

"Well it's a good thing you liked to stay up late," Danni said. " 'Cause I have a feeling it's one of the requirements for college — especialy with a roommate like Lacey."

Margot seemed to relax visibly."Yeah," she

said. "It's going to be pretty interesting, don't you think?"

"Definitely," said Danni. "Most definitely."

That night, Danni reached up to turn off her bed-lamp.

"G'night, Margot," she said.

Margot looked up from her careful scrutiny of her fingernails. "G'night," she said and smiled warmly at Danni.

I'm glad, thought Danni as she fell asleep contentedly, we're going to be friends. Good friends.

Margot stared sightlessly down at her fingernails, playing the past twenty-four hours over in her mind. It had been a good day. She'd made a couple of slips, talking to Danni about Lacey. And Cary Grant. That had been really embarrassing. Cary Grant was someone old people, like her mother, thought was cute.

But Danni didn't seem to have noticed, or if she had, she'd ignored it politely.

Careful, I have to be careful, Margot thought.

In the harsh overhead light of the bathroom, Lacey was putting down the seaweed face-masque she'd just applied. She grimaced at her green-masked face. What a jerk, she scolded herself silently. You want to get a rep or something?

Well, yes, said the voice in her head. The voice of her other self. Her bad self. Sometimes she and her bad self could have endless conversations. Sometimes her good self won. But sometimes her bad self did. Like last night. Or worse. . . .

"No," said Lacey, softly. "No." She bent and washed the mask off her face, scrubbing hard, as if she really were washing away all her impurities.

Going into her room and sliding into bed, Lacey heard Mouse roll over and sigh deeply in her sleep.

What did a mouse have to sigh about, wondered Lacey. How awful to lead a boring, mousey life!

Not that she wasn't bored herself. She turned restlessly in the dark. Bored. Ready for something exciting to happen. Ready for trouble.

Mouse murmured agitatedly.

"Mouse?" said Lacey softly.

Mouse's murmur subsided. She slept on.

Mouse. A mouse for a roommate. Lacey slid up on one elbow and stared through the dark at the darkened form sleeping across the room from her. She thought of Pete. Pete might be useful.

The spectre of boredom receded a bit, and she didn't stop to think whether it was her bad self or her good one that came with the idea.

Maybe it would be fun.

Yes.

Maybe it would be fun to play with a mouse.

Chapter 9

The days moved quickly now. Classes, as Lacey joked, began to interfere with everyone's social life. But Danni had no complaints. She'd never felt she belonged in a place so much as she belonged at Salem. The easy friendship of the others in the dormitory was all she had hoped for. There was always someone to talk to, to hang out with, no matter what time of day or night, and Danni soon felt she had known her roommates forever.

Best of all, Margot had responded to Danni's overtures of friendship at last. Margot was a private person who seldom talked about herself, but she had become more and more friendly.

In a way, it had been a help that Margot's clothes still hadn't arrived. Borrowing Danni's clothes had made Margot more trusting and approachable, despite her brusque thanks. She was always quick to offer to help Danni, whether with homework or getting snacks from the Dungeon vending machines. Often, too, Danni looked up from time to time to find Margot watching her. When Danni caught Margot's eyes at those moments, Margot would smile quickly and look away.

Maybe not the roommate she would have picked, exactly, but a good roommate, all the same. Anyone would agree, thought Danni. If only, thought Danni, I could get used to her.

Funny Margot.

Funny Margot, Danni thought, late one afternoon, pushing open the door to her room. At first she didn't realize anyone was there.

Then she saw funny Margot.

Sleeping in Danni's bed.

Danni's mouth dropped open. She could barely believe her eyes. But it was true.

Stretched out on top of Danni's bed, her hand resting on a book Danni had left there, Margot was sleeping.

What was she doing there?

A chill crept over Danni. How weird. How strange.

Suddenly funny Margot didn't seem quite so funny.

As if she sensed Danni's presence, Margot opened her eyes. For a moment they were glazed and confused. Then reason and consciousness came back.

Margot sat up hastily. "Danni. What are you doing here?"

"What are *you* doing *there*?" Danni answered.

"I-I must have fallen asleep." Margot jumped off Danni's bed and slid gingerly around Danni.

"But what were you doing there in the first place?"

"Nothing. I sat down to look at your — your book — and I must have fallen alseep, that's all."

"My chemistry book?" asked Danni.

"Probably why I fell asleep." Margot shrugged, not quite meeting Danni's eyes. Instead, she picked up her pack. "Want something from the Dungeon? I'm gonna head down there to study."

"No, thank you," Danni answered formally.

Margot didn't seem to notice. "Okay," she said cheerfully. "See you later."

Danni stood staring after her. Was she over-reacting?

Or was Margot as weird as Danni was beginning to believe she was?

Mouse, who had been trailing behind Lacey as they left class, shuffling through her lecture notes, jumped. "W-what?"

"You trust me, right, Mouse?"

"Trust *you*?"

"Did you hear anybody else ask you the question?" asked Lacey.

"No. I mean, no, I didn't hear anybody else . . ."

"Well, do you trust me or not?"

"Yes. I mean, I think I do."

"Good enough. I'm going to get my hair cut. You're coming, too."

"I am? But I was going to study," protested Mouse.

"You know how they say, think globally, act locally?"

"Yes . . ."

"Good," said Lacey. "I'm going to improve our environment by acting locally — with a Mouse makeover."

"No!" said Mouse, stopping dead in her tracks.

"Yes."

"But I . . . you can't . . . what . . ."

"You trust me, don't you? You weren't lying, were you?"

"Yes. No. I . . . you . . ."

A moment later, Lacey was hauling the still protesting Mouse across campus in the direction of the Strip nearby, where among the pizza parlors and fastfood joints and student bars and drug stores was also Salem Place Haircutters.

Shortly after that, still protesting feebly, Mouse was sitting in the chair, wrapped in a chartreuse smock. A woman clothed in a black smock, with hair shaved a quarter of an inch all over her skull and bleached white with black spots stepped up behind Mouse. The words *Leslie the haircutter* were embroidered on the pocket of the smock.

"What did you have in mind?" she asked, picking up a pair of scissors.

"Nothing!" squeaked Mouse, cringing away from the scissors.

"Put your hands over your ears, Mouse," ordered Lacey. "Leslie here has been known to cut ears off a mouse, right, Leslie?"

In answer, Leslie snapped the scissors suggestively. Mouse gasped and clapped her hands over her ears and closed her eyes.

"She needs style," said Lacey. "Nothing too radical, but . . ." Lacey waved her hands in the air.

"Gotcha," said Leslie the haircutter.

"Terrif," said Lacey, and she settled down in a nearby chair to watch.

Sometime later, Leslie stepped back triumphantly. "Check it out," she said.

Lacey got up and walked around Mouse's chair.

Mouse sat rigidly, frozen in place, her eyes wide.

"Nice," approved Lacey. "Very nice."

"How about a little color?" suggested Leslie.

Mouse's mouth opened but no sound came out. She'd been rendered speechless.

Lacey shook her head. "That's enough for right now."

At last Mouse found words. "My hair."

"You didn't need all that hair. Right, Leslie? You look fabulous, Mouse, absolutely fabulous."

"But — "

"Let's check back at the dorm. I think Danni and Margot should be part of this next stage."

"But — "

"Come on!"

* * *

Danni yawned and looked up from her book. What she saw startled her. She made a choking sound.

Without opening her eyes, Margot said, "Mmm?"

"Margot, do you see what I see?"

"I don't know," said Margot. "My eyes are closed."

"Open them!" chortled Lacey, and pushed Mouse ahead of her through the door of room 2B.

Obediently, Margot opened her eyes. She focused on Lacey, and then on the person with Lacey. She sat up abruptly. "Mouse? Is that you?"

Mouse's hands went up to cover her ears, but Lacey caught her by the wrists. "Cut that out. You look great! Doesn't she?"

Still staring, Margot got up to inspect Mouse more closely. At last she nodded. "It's the truth, Mouse."

"So now I'm thinking the mall, right?" said Lacey. "Makeup, the right clothes, the works!"

Danni laughed. "Count me in."

"Me, too," said Margot.

"Good," said Lacey.

"Oh, nooo," wailed Mouse.

It was soon clear Mouse wasn't used to shopping with friends.

"Girl, haven't you ever seen a mall before?" asked Lacey, as she ruthlessly herded Mouse into the dressing room of one store after another. In one store, there was just one big dressing room, lined with mirrors and people undressing and dressing while studying their reflections. Mouse backed into a mirrored corner and began to struggle vainly to get dressed and undressed without flashing any skin. At last Lacey gave a growl of exasperation, and almost ripped a sweater off over Mouse's head.

"Oh!" cried Mouse.

Danni felt a flash of sympathy for the hapless Mouse. But it was for a good cause, she reminded herself.

At last they were finished, right down to ordering a new pair of glasses for Mouse and having her fitted with contact lenses. Lacey was lecturing Mouse on the importance of the right look as they staggered out from the mall under the load of all their new purchases and headed for the bus stop.

"Wow, I thought we were gonna melt the plastic on your credit cards there for a while, Mouse. What do you think? How does the world look through rose-colored contacts? Not that you should forget your glasses. The right glasses can be very distinctive. Very, very distinctive."

Danni tapped her finger against her chin and smiled. She looked up to find Margot watching. Margot smiled, too.

"You didn't buy anything, Margot," said Danni. "We all bought gear but you."

Margot shrugged. "It doesn't mean I don't love to shop."

"Tell me about it," said Lacey.

Danni said, "I guess you're not an impulse buyer."

"I bet Margot doesn't have an impulsive bone in her body," said Lacey.

"I admit it, Lacey," said Margot. "I lack your — spontaneous qualities."

"Look at Danni, on the other hand," Lacey went on. "She did an excellent shopping workout. Although it *hurts* me to see someone pay *cash*. Danni, my woman, haven't you ever heard of plastic?"

Danni laughed. "Cash spends just as good, don't you think?"

"True," said Lacey. "And no nasty records of how much you spent where, so your parents can hunt you down and kill you. Or worse, make you return something. . . ."

That made all the girls crack up laughing. Except Margot, Danni noticed who had a mysterious look on her face.

She loved clothes. Silk and linen, soft cotton and smooth wool. Materials woven with metallic threads. Velvet. Cashmere. Lambswool . . .

She loved Lacey's clothes. And Danni's. She was drawn to them as if they were magic. Sometimes, when they weren't there, when no one was home in the suite, she would open their drawers and touch the silk, smooth the cashmere yearningly, press her cheek against the softness.

Of course, she couldn't let them catch her. They'd never understand. How could they? The only way to make them understand would be to tell them the truth.

And she couldn't do that.

That would be fatal.

Danni opened her drawer and frowned.

The Salem University chimes gave the single toll that meant it was ten minutes before the hour. She was going to be late.

Great. The second week of classes and she was already late.

Where was the gold sweater?

"I know you're here somewhere," she muttered, then stopped herself. She was starting to sound like Mouse.

At least no one had heard her. The suite was quiet. Lacey, for all her insistence that she was a terrible student and hated studying, had long since left for her Intro Psych course. Mouse had departed soon after, murmuring anxiously about the library. Margot had simply disappeared before Danni had awakened.

Margot. Had Margot taken the sweater?

How could she? Danni felt a flash of anger. How could Margot, who had practically threatened Danni's life for touching Margot's belongings, have taken Danni's sweater without asking?

Calm down, Danni, she told herself. Margot's clothes haven't gotten here yet. You probably just weren't around when Margot needed it.

Yes, that was probably it.

Danni tried to shake the sense of unease it gave her — the thought of Margot going through her drawers, touching her things.

Don't be silly, she scolded herself. It's not like I'm compulsively neat like Mouse. And it's not like I don't have almost as many clothes as Lacey.

Two minutes, she thought suddenly. You have two minutes before class.

Putting the thought of Margot going through her drawers out of her mind, Danni put on a lambswool turtleneck and raced out of the room.

When Danni and Lacey got back from class that afternoon, Margot was sitting at her desk, studying. She was wearing Danni's gold cashmere sweater.

"Margot."

Margot looked up slowly from her book, obviously distracted. "Mmm?"

"Margot, you remember what happened the first day you were here?" Danni asked.

As Margot frowned, Lacey wandered over to the bulletin board above Danni's desk, and seemed to become absorbed in the melange of clippings and photos and mementos there.

Slowly Margot nodded. "I was late. What about it?"

"The next day," Danni said. "I was standing by your chest of drawers. The letter opener was there, remember?"

Margot looked quickly over at the chest of

drawers. "It still is. What about it?"

"You told me never, ever to touch anything of yours, remember?"

"Did I?" said Margot. She gave an uncertain little laugh. "I was probably strung out from not sleeping. You know."

"Margot, that's *my* sweater," Danni blurted out.

Margot looked down. Unconsciously, she raised one hand to stroke the soft sleeve. "So?"

"So why are you wearing it?"

The stroking motion continued, but now Margot was staring at Danni. "What do you mean?"

"Why are you wearing my sweater," repeated Danni, "without even asking to borrow it? It's not that I mind. But after you practically threatened my life when I touched that old letter opener of yours, don't you think — "

She never got to finish. Margot jumped up so suddenly that the chair in which she'd been sitting fell over with a crash. In one bound she was across the room, her face up close to Danni's.

Danni shrank back. "M-Margot?"

Margot's eyes were blazing. "What did you say?"

"Margot, it's okay. I was just — "

"You told me I could *have* the sweater," said Margot.

For one moment, Danni was so astonished she forgot to be scared. "I didn't. I never said that!"

"Are you accusing me of lying?" The last word came out in a hiss.

"No! No, but you might have misunderstood — "

"Of stealing, then?"

"No, Margot. Margot, NOOO!"

Margot had snatched the letter opener. Danni flung herself back against the wall, her hands in front of her face. "No, no, no," she moaned.

Lacey grabbed Margot's wrist from behind, but Margot shook her off as easily as if Lacey were a feather.

"Is this your way of paying me back, Danni?" asked Margot with sudden, frightening calm, holding the letter opener out.

"Why? For w-what?" gasped Danni.

"For telling you to ask before touching my things? Was that your plan? Give me your sweater, then call me a liar? A thief? Humiliate me in front of Lacey?"

"That's crazy!" said Danni.

"Crazy? As crazy as pretending to be my friend, wouldn't you say?"

"I *am* your friend, Margot. I'm sorry, it's all a misunderstanding!" Danni's last word ended in a shriek of terror as Margot pulled back her arm and threw the letter opener.

But Margot turned at the last minute. The letter opener spun end over end and landed, point down, in the soft, scarred wood top of the dresser. It quivered there for a moment, then slowly fell over and clattered into silence.

In horrified silence Danni and Lacey watched as Margot stripped the gold sweater off over her head.

"Margot, please," pleaded Danni. "You can keep the sweater. It's all been a misunderstanding."

"I don't need your friendship! And I don't want your charity," retorted Margot. With shaking fingers she folded the sweater. She walked toward Danni, her eyes blazing.

Danni shrank back against Lacey.

"Here," said Margot. She thrust the sweater into Danni's arms so hard that Danni felt as if she'd been punched in the stomach. Then Margot stalked out of the room.

"Oh, wow," said Lacey, more loudly. "I

mean, Margot went nuclear. That was amazing. Like she went berserk. She's got a temper, y'know."

Danni knew. She'd stared into Margot's blazing eyes. It was frightening, the rage she'd seen.

"She's crazy, Lacey," whispered Danni. "My roommate is crazy."

Chapter 10

Lacey glanced over her shoulder. She had the strangest feeling she was being followed. Watched.

It was not a new feeling. Lately, however, it had been worse. Much worse. And since that scene between Margot and Danni, the feeling had intensified. She was almost afraid to look in the mirror. Afraid she'd see the reflection of someone behind her.

Watching.

Waiting.

Chill, Lacey, she told herself. It's just some cute, shy guy. Yeah, that was it. Had to be.

The towers chimed ten minutes before the hour and people began spilling out of the various buildings around the Commons. According to Lacey's calculations, she was right on time to put her plan in motion. She crossed the terrace of the Student Center and sat down on the low stone wall next to Mouse, who was huddled over a long, handwritten piece of paper in one hand, a hastily torn-open envelope in the other.

"Love letters?" inquired Lacey.

Mouse jumped and involuntarily crumpled the paper in her hand. "Oh! Lacey! You startled me."

"Surprise is the essence of the successful attack," murmured Lacey.

Her eyes round, Mouse said, "Wh-what?"

"You look good," said Lacey. "At the risk of sounding like your mother — or *someone's* mother, anyway, sit up straight and act like you know it."

Obedience seemed to be a reflex action in Mouse, thought Lacey as Mouse straightened up. If I didn't know better, I'd think she was a well-trained inmate from some kind of institution.

Lacey turned casually. She was being watched for sure now, but by someone she knew. Someone she knew would be on his way back from class, walking by where they were sitting, at this very moment.

"Pete!" Lacey waved and a minute later Pete had sauntered up the steps onto the terrace to join them. He was with his friend Ian Banion, a photographer for the school paper. Explaining he had a class, Ian took off.

Lacey scooted to one side and patted the wall between her and Mouse invitingly. Pete sat down.

"What are you doing here?" asked Lacey innocently, as if she hadn't known Pete would be walking by.

"Just finished class. Thought I'd check my mail," said Pete easily.

"That's what Mous — Maureen has just been doing, wasn't it, Maureen?"

"What?" said Mouse.

"You just went to the PO and got a letter, right? Oh, Pete! I'm sorry. Have you met my roomie yet?"

"No," said Pete as Mouse began to blush and duck her head. Then she caught Lacey's eye, blushed even harder, but sat up straight.

"Maureen, this is Pete. He was at the party the other night at the Kennel. He's the sports editor for *The Chronicle*."

"Hi," said Pete. "I don't remember seeing you at the party."

"Maureen had to leave early," said Lacey quickly.

They both looked at Mouse. *Say something,*

Mouse, Lacey thought, trying to convey the order with her eyes.

At last Mouse said shyly, "I like sports."

Oh, *feeble*, Mouse, thought Lacey, groaning inwardly. But Pete didn't seem to notice. "Me, too," he said grinning. "Good thing, huh?"

Unexpectedly, Mouse laughed.

Danni's right, thought Lacey, remembering what Danni had said about how Mouse became a completely different person when she smiled. The Mouse who was smiling shyly up at Pete was almost — beautiful. Especially, thought Lacey, with my Mouse makeover.

Pete said, "Was the school newspaper part of your extracurricular, won't-it-look-good-on-my-college-application schtick in high school?"

"*Schtick?*" Mouse repeated.

"Act, program. You know, the things that make you look good to the college admissions board."

"Well, I was on the newspaper. . . ."

"Mo — Maureen is a good writer, too. I've seen her work," Lacey interposed.

"You have?" Mouse's expression changed. A panicked look came over her face. "What do you mean? What are you talking about?"

"It was on your desk. I was looking for a pencil. Same dif," said Lacey airily.

"What did you see? Tell me," Mouse demanded frantically.

"Relax. Your secrets are safe with me," Lacey said.

"But . . ." began Mouse.

"Maybe you should try out for *The Chronicle*," suggested Pete.

"Great idea," said Lacey.

Mouse seemed to be struggling for words, her eyes fixed on Lacey. Ignoring what Lacey was beginning to recognize as Mouse's signs of incipient panic, Lacey rushed on. "Where do you sign up, or whatever it is you do?"

"I'm headed that way myself. I can explain it on our way over if you'd like," Pete said, looking at Mouse.

"Great," said Lacey, seizing Mouse's elbow and pulling her to her feet. "Listen, I've got to motor. I'll catch you guys later."

"Lacey," Mouse said in an agonized voice.

Lacey gave Mouse a warning look. "Terrif. See ya," and she hurried away before Mouse could escape.

"She's a piece of work, isn't she?" asked Pete, nodding in the direction Lacey had gone. "You guys must be pretty good roommates, though."

Remembering her letter, Mouse smoothed it

out with shaking hands, then folded it and thrust it into her book. She was too dazed to answer. First the makeover and now this. What was Lacey trying to do to her?

Pete didn't seem to notice Mouse's distraction. "I mean I can tell you're kind of opposites." Pete began to walk off the terrace and toward Bly Hall, the journalism building. "I mean, Lacey is a party animal, but you seem quieter, more serious."

"I guess you could say that," Mouse answered cautiously.

Pete smiled at Mouse. She met his eyes and he looked so friendly and kind. Not scary at all. Almost unwittingly, she smiled back.

Pete's smile widened and for a moment, Mouse felt weightless. Could he like me? Could someone like Pete like me?

Then she realized she was still staring up at Pete and she began to blush.

Clearing his throat, Pete said, "We're almost there. Anyway, like I was saying, you must be pretty good roommates. You and Lacey seem to get along. But look at me now, I've got the roommate from hell."

They mounted the steps of Bly Hall. "Second floor, turn left," Pete said. "Not that I don't like Jordan, but he's kinda . . ." Pete hesitated.

"Danni, one of my roommates, she's gone out with a guy named Jordan."

"Really?" Pete raised his eyebrows.

Mouse waited for Pete to say more, but he didn't.

"What is it about Jordan?" asked Mouse. "What were you going to say?"

"Nothing," said Pete harshly. Then, catching sight of Mouse's startled expression, he shook his head. "Nothing," he said more calmly.

Before Mouse could ask any more questions, Pete pushed open a door at the end of the hall and motioned Mouse through with a flourish. She stepped inside, and stopped abruptly. All she could do was stare. The room was filled with a jumble of desks, chairs, computers, bulletin boards, and, on a far wall, a dart board. Stacks of papers were everywhere, from computer printouts to newspapers. Photographs and newsclippings were tacked and taped to every wall surface in the room that wasn't covered by bulletin boards or posters. Phones were ringing. Two people were shouting at each other. A young woman wearing grubby jeans and an ancient, funky sweatshirt was leaning precariously back in a chair with her eyes closed and a dart in her hand. As they watched, she drew her arm back and threw the dart. It landed nowhere near the dart board, but stuck fast in the windowframe.

It was then that Mouse noticed the sign on the desk in front of the young woman. It said, THE EDITOR IS IN with *sane* written on a piece of paper and taped next to the word "IN."

"Welcome to *The Chronicle*," said Pete. "I think you're going to like it."

Margot finished addressing the envelope. It was a fat envelope. It had taken two stamps to send first class. But the letter had been a long one. Full of love and promises. Full of praise and support. The perfect letter for the perfect daughter of a perfect family.

With a flourish, she dropped the letter into the mailbox and turned.

Danni was standing just outside the campus post office door. She was staring at something that Margot couldn't see. Seeing Danni, Margot felt the humiliation burning through her veins. How could Danni have accused her — and in front of Lacey. . . .

And yet, Danni looked so graceful, standing there. As if Salem University were just some unreal setting, as if she were a star who didn't even belong there.

Maybe Margot would forgive her. Although it would be nice to make her pay. But Danni was so pretty. She had so much to give. Even if she didn't know it.

Yet.

Danni turned. Her eyes met Margot's.

Margot turned on her heel and walked away, pleased at the momentary surprise that she'd seen on Danni's face, the momentary surprise followed by the quick look of fear.

Yes, maybe she would forgive Danni. Or at least make a good show of it.

Danni smoothed the last shirt from her laundry over the coat hanger and aligned it with the rest of the shirts at one end of her closet.

"You're as bad as Mouse," complained Lacey, who was in her characteristic horizontal position, this time on the rug by Danni's bed.

As if on cue the door to room 2A banged open.

"Lacey!"

"Hmmm," said Lacey to the ceiling. "Does my roomie sound P.O.'d? Mad? Mad enough to kill?"

Danni, who'd been laughing helplessly at Lacey's wicked description of the meeting between Mouse and Pete on the terrace that afternoon said, "Don't be crazy, Lacey. Why would she be mad? Besides, Mouse hasn't got what it takes to lose her temper."

"Everyone's capable of murder," answered Lacey with calm certainty.

The bathroom door flew open. "Lacey! There you are!"

"Yeah, Mouse, here I am. So, are you trying out for the newspaper or what?"

Mouse blushed, but she nodded vigorously. "I am. Pete," she paused, blushing harder, but obviously relishing saying his name aloud, "said he thought I'd have a good chance."

"Excellent," said Lacey. "What about your chance of making the newspaper?"

It took Mouse a moment to get that. Then she gave Lacey a look that was both terrified and defiant. "Oh, Lacey. Pete *couldn't* like someone like me. Besides, *you* like him. Don't you?"

"After all the work I've done, this is the thanks I get?" asked Lacey.

Mouse looked bewildered.

Lacey went on languidly, "He's all yours. You win. I give up."

How cruel, thought Danni. Lacey was such a contradiction. Going to all that trouble to help

Mouse, and now torturing her. Just like a cat.

Echoing Danni's thoughts, Mouse said timidly, "You helped me a lot, Lacey. But why have you done all this for me? I really appreciate it. I don't want to seem ungrateful. But why?"

"Don't bore me," said Lacey, sitting up abruptly. "You haven't got anything to be grateful for. I have my reasons."

"Don't you like Pete?" asked Mouse.

"I like Pete. But I like a hundred other guys, too, okay?" Lacey made an elaborate show of yawning. Then she switched her attention to Danni.

"So, Danni. Seen your friendly roommate lately?"

"No," Danni answered softly, remembering the last, painful meeting in the post office. "Not really. She leaves before I get up in the morning. Comes home late at night."

"She's doing the avoiding-you-like-the-plague thing, huh? Too bad. She seemed to admire you so much at first."

Danni didn't answer.

Without warning, Lacey bounded to her feet and pulled open Margot's closet door. Very little was inside.

"Don't, Lacey," said Danni.

Lacey closed the door and looked inquiringly at Danni. "Don't what?"

"Don't go through other people's stuff like that."

"Why not, Danni?"

"I don't know." Danni was reluctant to tell Lacey that it gave her the creeps, that she felt so stupidly possessive about her things.

But with her uncanny perceptiveness, Lacey had already figured it out. She smiled slowly. "You don't mind Margot borrowing the sweater. You just don't like her opening your drawers, looking in your closets."

"Puh-lease," said Danni, forcing a note of lightness she didn't feel into her voice.

"You don't like her or anyone touching what's yours. That's it, right?" pressed Lacey.

Danni made herself meet Lacey's eyes and the two stared at each other for a long moment. Then Lacey said, "Well, anyway, we know that Margot's things haven't gotten here yet."

"Maybe they got lost," suggested Mouse.

The three roommates were silent for a moment, contemplating the horrors of losing all their clothes to the great god of airlines, or trains, or buses.

Then Lacey laughed. "Think of it! All new

clothes. Kind of like your stuff, Danni."

"I take good care of my clothes, Lacey," said Danni, frowning. Had *Lacey* been going through her closet, her drawers?

Mouse said unexpectedly, "You went through *my* stuff, Lacey."

"When?" asked Lacey.

"When you read that paper on my desk. Remember, you told Pete and me you'd been looking for a pencil. What did you find?"

Lacey strolled deliberately back to the rug and resettled herself in her horizontal position before answering. "I was looking for a pencil, *okay*, Mouse?"

"What did you find on my desk, Lacey? *What did you read?*" Mouse demanded.

Danni and Lacey looked at Mouse in astonishment.

Then Lacey said, "Well, the words 'sexual expression' kinda leaped off the paper at me. How could I not read it?"

Danni's eyes widened. " 'Sexual expression'?"

Looking wildly around, Mouse said, "It was for Psych. A paper for my Psych class."

"Mouse. Girlfriend. *I* take Psych 101 and that is not a topic that has come up. Believe me, I'd know."

"Hey, Mouse, are you holding out on us?" asked Danni.

"Yeah," Lacey said. "Like are you some kind of wild and crazy person and you forgot to tell us?"

"No! No," said Mouse. "No. It's for Advanced Psych, that's all."

"You *are* holding out on us," Danni said. Lacey was watching Mouse closely.

"No. I took a test and they placed me in Advanced Psych. I'm the only first-year student in there."

Lacey whistled softly, never taking her eyes off Mouse. "What else are holding out on us about, Mouse?"

"Nothing!"

"Nothing? Nothing at all? Are you sure?"

"No. Yes! I mean . . ." Mouse took a deep breath. "My parents are both psychiatrists. I can't help it."

"Don't apologize, Mouse, it's cool," said Danni, although she couldn't imagine anything more repulsive than having shrinks for parents. Creepy, even.

Margot still hadn't returned when Danni went to bed. I hate this, she thought. She tried to make herself stay awake. She wanted to apologize, to explain. Maybe she had said something that Margot had misunderstood. Had she?

But how could she have? Wouldn't she have remembered?

She must have fallen asleep. The next thing she knew the phone that hung on the bathroom wall was ringing. She stumbled out of bed and into the bathroom, thinking as she had before, "What a stupid place to put the phone. Why can't we have phones in our rooms? It was probably for Lacey, anyhow."

"Hello?" she whispered.

No answer.

"Hello? Hello, who is it?"

And then she heard. A tiny, distant breath. A sigh.

"Danni, is that you?"

"Who is this?"

"I know who you are."

"Who are you?"

"I know who you are, Danni. Better than anyone. I'm your friend. Friends should spend time together, Danni. But you've been a bad friend, Danni."

"Who is this? WHO ARE YOU?"

"Very, very bad. And now you have to be punished."

As the line went dead, Danni dropped the receiver. She pressed her fists against her mouth and backed up. "No," she whispered. "No, no, no. . . ."

And hands came out of the darkness and grabbed her.

Chapter 11

Danni screamed. She screamed and screamed. She couldn't stop screaming.

Light flooded the bedroom. She saw her roommates in the bathroom doorway. Struggling free of the hands, she spun around.

Margot stood there, her face pale, the door to room 2A open behind her.

Up and down the hall, doors were opening. A moment later, Kendra hurried into the room. "What is going on here? Danni? Margot?"

"I don't know!" said Margot sharply. "How would I know? Don't look at me. I just got here. I swear I did."

"You grabbed me!" Danni choked out.

Kendra seemed to become aware of the others who lived on the hall trying to peer in the door around her. "Okay, okay, that's enough.

Everybody go back to sleep or whatever you were doing. Go on now."

With murmurings and curious glances, everyone slowly, reluctantly dispersed. Kendra turned back around and pulled the door shut behind her.

"What happened here?" she demanded.

"I'm sorry!" Margot said to Danni. "I came in and you were standing there and I guess I reached out and grabbed you. You were backing up . . . I thought you were going to bump into me and I didn't want to scare you."

"Scare me? *Scare me!*" Danni began hysterically.

"What were you doing up?" asked Kendra. "Were you having a nightmare? Do you sleepwalk?"

"No. No." For a moment, she almost believed that it had been a nightmare, that a dreadful, soft voice had never whispered her name over the phone. But it had.

"There was a phone call . . . I answered. Someone . . . said my name. They said I was bad. That I was going to be p-punished."

"Wow," breathed Lacey. "Just like one of those movies."

"Lacey," said Kendra sharply.

"I didn't hear the phone ring," said Mouse,

frowning. "I didn't hear anything until I heard Danni screaming. Then I jumped up and followed Lacey in here to see what had happened."

Kendra looked at Lacey, who looked disappointed. "I didn't, either," she admitted reluctantly. "But I can sleep through anything."

"Someone called me," said Danni. "He did! He did. He threatened me."

"Okay, okay," said Kendra soothingly. "Why don't you come down to my room for a little while and we'll talk about this. If you're getting threatening calls, we need to file some kind of report with campus security. And — "

Danni shook her head, imagining what people would say. "No. No, I don't want to do that."

Kendra looked exasperated. "Why not?"

Danni looked around helplessly. Suddenly her eyes met Margot's.

"I understand," said Margot, quickly. "You just want to forget about it."

"Yes, yes, that's it," said Danni gratefully.

Kendra shook her head. "I think you're making a mistake. If you change your mind, let me know."

The four roommates stood silently as Kendra left.

"*Wow*," said Lacey softly. "I never had a guy calling me up like that. Evil, Danni. Like that movie, *Fatal Attraction*, y'know?"

Margot's face had gotten very pale. "Do you think someone followed you? Some guy you had a romance with in high school?"

"No!" cried Danni. "It's not . . . it's not possible."

"Maybe it was a nightmare," offered Mouse.

"Maybe it was," said Danni. "And maybe it wasn't."

Chapter 12

"Danni?"

It was the voice again. It was coming to get her.

She tried to turn away.

"Danni?" A whisper. An obscene hiss . . .

"NO!" Danni bolted upright in her bed.

Margot, who had been standing beside her, leaped back.

"Get away from me!" gasped Danni.

"I'm sorry! I'm sorry!" said Margot. "I was just trying to wake you up. You were having a nightmare."

Dazed, her heart pounding, Danni looked around the room. It was very early, the gray light of dawn. The things in the room — the bathrobe flung across the foot of her bed, the pile of books on her desk, the scattering of jewelry and makeup across the top of her chest of drawers, the vividly colored posters, all had an ordinary look, neatly messy, lived in.

For a moment Danni's eyes lingered on Margot's side of the room. It, too, had a pile of books on the desk, a bathrobe hung over the back of the desk chair, a watch and a necklace on the top of the chest of drawers. But it was more barren, somehow, than Danni's. No photographs. No mementos from high school stuck up on the bulletin board.

"Danni?" asked Margot tentatively, from a safe distance across the room.

Danni took a harsh breath. "What?"

"I'm sorry. Sorry about the misunderstanding. I appreciate your letting me borrow your sweater, really I do. If you'll let me have it, I'll take it to get it cleaned and then give it back to you. I really did — I must have misunderstood you — "

"Sweater?" Danni had almost forgotten the sweater. She frowned and her head began to ache.

"Will you forgive me, Danni? About the sweater? I — I want us to be friends. To go on being friends."

Why did her head hurt so badly? And why was she so tired? So tired.

"Danni?" Margot repeated.

"Okay," said Danni. "It's okay, Margot."

"Are you sure?"

Danni forced herself to smile. "Sure. Don't worry."

"Thanks." Margot smiled back in relief. "Listen, I've got to leave. Can I get you anything before I go?"

"No, thanks," said Danni. "I'm not an invalid, you know."

"No, but . . ." Margot trailed off, studying Danni intently. Then she nodded. "Okay. But if you need anything, you let me know."

"How about the answers to the next Art History quiz?" Danni joked feebly. "Know anything about Hieronymus Bosch?"

Laughing, Margot gathered up her books and pack. "Now there's a *real* nightmare," she said.

She was gone before Danni could answer. Before Danni could say, what do you mean, *real* nightmare? My nightmare *was* real. Why doesn't anyone believe me? It was real.

Wasn't it?

The next few days passed in a blur. For a while, Danni thought her headache would never go away. It made it hard for her to think, to concentrate in class, to remember what anyone said to her. It was even affecting her social life.

And the nightmare wouldn't go away. Without any effort at all she could conjure up the soft menacing voice whispering into the telephone.

Especially when it happened again.

This time, she was all alone in the suite, wandering restlessly around after her last class, wishing someone would come home so she'd have someone to talk to. She hated being alone.

She was just about to go down the hall to Jodie and Caren's when the phone rang.

Danni froze. For a long minute she listened to it ring.

Then she gave herself a mental shake. It wasn't even dark outside, she told herself. It was just someone calling for Lacey or Mouse or Margot. Or maybe Jordan, calling for her.

That's all.

With shaking hands she lifted the receiver.

"Danni, can you hear me?"

"No," whispered Danni. A shudder went through her body.

"I can hear you, Danni. See you. I know everything about you."

"No!" cried Danni.

"We'll be together again soon, Danni. Soooooon."

"NOOOO!" Danni threw down the receiver and reeled out of the bathroom to collapse on her bed.

Chapter 13

"Ha, ha, ha, ha!"

"You've got to be kidding!"

"No, really! Hey, Danni. . . . Danni?" Margot stopped laughing abruptly, the first of the three roommates who had come into the room to realize that something was very, very wrong with Danni. "Danni, what's wrong?"

"The phone call. The phone call. He called me again . . ." gasped Danni, trying not to cry.

Lacey went over and lifted the receiver from the floor, where it was dangling from the end of its cord. She held it to her ear and shook her head.

"No one there," Lacey said, and hung up the phone.

"He hung up, then," said Danni.

Margot patted Danni's shoulder soothingly.

Danni looked from one face to the other.

None of them believed her. She could tell. Why wouldn't they believe her?

"Why don't you believe me?" she cried.

"We do, we do," Margot said. But her tone belied the words.

Lacey looked thoughtful. "Hey, it's a secret admirer, right? What did he say?"

But when Danni told them, it seemed they believed her even less.

"It doesn't sound so scary," said Lacey.

"Wait till it happens to you!" said Danni.

"I'd report it if it happened to me," said Lacey.

"You really should," added Mouse.

"No!" said Danni. "I — I don't want people to know."

"Why not, Danni?" asked Margot.

"They'll think I'm weird. They'll — I don't want people talking about me."

"Well, that's the dif between you and me," said Lacey, with a cackle.

"Oh, Lacey!" said Mouse, but she smiled, while Margot shook her head ruefully.

"Listen, let's go get dinner or something. Forget about all this," suggested Margot.

"It's Friday night!" said Lacey. "We've all got dates. Don't we?"

Margot smiled. "A study date — me and the library."

"Pete and I are meeting at the library to talk about the newspaper," said Mouse.

"Yeah, yeah, sure," said Lacey. "Me, I've got a date, with Travis."

"Not your type," teased Margot.

"Every type is my type," Lacey retorted.

"Well, don't worry about me," said Danni loudly. "I'll just stay here and. . . ."

The phone rang again.

Lacey swooped down on it and snatched it up. She listened a moment, then turned to Danni. "It's for you."

"No," said Danni. "No!"

"Danni, it's Jordan."

"Jordan," repeated Danni blankly. Feeling foolish, she got slowly to her feet and took the phone from Lacey. She bent her head and said softly, "Hello?"

"Ready?" said a voice at the other end.

For a moment Danni panicked. She forced herself to calm down, to say in a reasonable tone, "Jordan?"

"Who else, babes? The movies, remember? *Psycho* at the Student Center."

"What?"

Jordan said, "You haven't forgotten? You

said you *loved* those kinds of movies."

"I did?" She couldn't remember saying anything like that.

"Danni!" He sounded half-amused, half-impatient.

Pulling herself together, Danni said, "Jordan, I'm not quite ready, okay?"

"Oh. Hey, no problem. I like sitting down here in the girls' dorm. Take your time."

Danni made herself laugh. "See you in five."

"Great." Jordan hung up.

Mouse poked her head around the bathroom door, then walked into the room. "How do I look, Danni?"

"Two thumbs up, right?" asked Lacey's voice from behind Mouse, and she and Margot followed Mouse into the room.

Mouse was in brown, but it was an arrangement in brown that somehow suited her, from the plain body suit with the scoop neck to the skirt splashed with red and brown and gold and purple, to the brown suede boots with the wicked heels. The new haircut made her thick hair look sleek and easy and seemed to bring out the red highlights in it.

"Definitely two thumbs up," said Danni. Her shakiness had left her. "We are talking *date* here, aren't we?"

"Just doing some work on *The Chronicle*," said Mouse, and Lacey gave her a knowing leer.

"I'll walk you over," said Margot. "The sooner I get started on that paper, the better."

"Danni, you have a date with Jordan, don't you?" Mouse asked as she opened the door.

"Yes," said Danni. "Why?"

"Nothing. It's just Pete started to tell me something about Jordan. But then he suddenly shut up."

Danni looked at Mouse curiously, but Mouse just shrugged. "I'm sure it was no big deal," she said, and headed back into her room.

Danni knew she should just ignore what Mouse had said.

But why had Mouse mentioned it? And . . . what was Pete going to say about Jordan?

"These movies are gross," Danni told Jordan, a few hours later as they were leaving the movie theater.

"Classic, the word is classic," Jordan said.

"You really like them?"

"Definitely. Expecially the ones with crazy people who try to act normal," Jordan told her. "This is one of my favorites. Good and scary."

"Ugh," said Danni, shuddering. Talking

about crazy people reminded her of the phone calls she'd received. Whoever had made them was definitely crazy. Weren't they?

Danni looked over her shoulder uneasily. It was ridiculous, she knew. But she couldn't shake the feeling she was being watched. Followed.

"Hello in there?" Jordan waved his hand in front of Danni's face. "I know I'm exciting and all," he continued. "But I didn't mean to overwhelm you into a coma, or anything."

"Sorry. Just thinking."

"See? I bring out the best in everybody!" said Jordan. "What do you want to do now?"

"What do you want to do?" Danni asked.

"Walk this way," said Jordan, and, catching her hand, he pulled her toward the shadows of the garden next to Griswold, the Salem U. science department building. The shape of something huge and menacing loomed up. Danni gasped and tried to pull her hand free.

"Hey, it's okay," said Jordan. "It's the science garden. The topiary garden, it's called. It's for art majors who aren't so good at science. One of the courses is sort of Basic Biology meets How to Make Your Trees and Shrubs Look Like Animals."

Looking more closely, Danni saw that the

bush in front of her was shaped like a giant rabbit.

Danni peered around her through the darkness. Beyond the rabbit, she saw other figures scattered across the grass, big and little, every shape and size. In the half-light that fell over the hedges enclosing the garden, they all looked surrealistic and somehow spooky. Even the rabbit didn't look particularly friendly. What six-foot rabbit would? she thought wryly.

Aloud she said, "Cool. I've never seen anything like these before. Where do you sign up for this course?"

No one answered.

"Jordan?" Danni said.

"Danniii."

It was a breath, a whisper, as frightening as the sound of a footfall in a house you thought was deserted.

No, she thought. Not Jordan.

"Jordan!"

No answer.

"Jordan, this isn't funny! Where are you?"

"Danni."

She whirled toward the sound — a normal-sounding whisper this time. She must have imagined the first.

"Jordan, this is a dumb game. World-class

dumb." She walked forward, then stopped. She was surrounded by fantastic shapes. Distorted shadows striped the grass. Where was the exit?

She looked back, but she couldn't see it. All she could see were topiary figures sitting motionless as tomb markers on the grass.

And then she saw one of them move.

Chapter 14

Danni turned blindly. Which way was out?

Blundering forward, she ran into the arms of a bear, shaped so it was sitting on its haunches.

"Let me go," she gasped, twisting in the scratchy branches.

The bear didn't move. Danni stumbled back and ran down another path.

"Danni."

She didn't hear the voice that time. In blind fear she turned left and then right, frantically seeking a way out.

Hands caught her shoulders.

"NOOOO!" she screamed. "Let me go, let me *go*!"

"Danni! Danni, stop it!"

Jordan caught her in his arms and pulled her

close. She struggled vainly for a moment, then lay still against him, trembling.

"Danni," he whispered into her hair and she froze.

It was the voice from the telephone.

"It was you!" she cried.

Jordan shook his head. "God, I'm sorry, Danni. I didn't know it would scare you like that. It was really stupid of me. A stupid joke. Dead wrong."

"You didn't mean to scare me? Are you crazy?"

"No! I get carried away sometimes. Bad habit, practical jokes. I've been trying to kick it and all . . ." He looked sheepishly away.

She jerked loose. "You creep! You think a threatening phone call is a practical joke?"

"What? What are you talking about?"

"That phone call the other night — Wednesday night. And tonight. That was you, wasn't it? 'Danni, I'm waiting for you. Danni, I'm coming to get you'?" she mimicked savagely.

"What! I don't know what you're talking about! I'd never do something like that. That's sick!"

"Well, you just said you liked sick, right? Sick movies. Sick people who try to act normal."

Jordan stepped back a pace and held up his hands. "Hey, slow down. Practical jokes are poor form, okay, I admit it. But practical jokes — and even liking horror movies — doesn't make me some kind of pervert. I would *never*, *ever*, call someone up and threaten them over the phone. Especially someone I liked . . ."

Danni peered at Jordan through the shadows. It was hard to tell what he was thinking. His face was hard to see.

She took a deep, shaky breath. "How do we get out of this place?" she asked.

"This way," said Jordan. He held out his hand.

Danni stared down at it.

"Peace, okay?" said Jordan. "I promise never, ever to play a joke like that on you again."

"I don't know," Danni said softly.

"Please, Danni? Give me another chance. Please?"

He sounded so sincere. So earnest. Against her better judgment she slowly reached out and took his hand.

"Okay," she said. "But it's late. I want to go home."

"Anything you want," said Jordan. "*Anything.*"

I must be losing my mind, thought Danni as she climbed the stairs to the fourth floor of her dorm. These things happen. Everyone makes goof calls when they're kids. Everyone's gotten them. Lacey, Mouse, Margot. And now me.

I just got a late start.

It's okay, she told herself. It's okay.

Danni, the voice had said. Whoever it was knew her name.

Stop it, Danni told herself. You're getting paranoid. It was just some crank call. They could've gotten your name from anywhere.

And more importantly, she'd established it wasn't Jordan. Not, she thought smiling faintly to herself, if his good-night kiss was any indication.

No, not Jordan. Not anybody she knew.

Just some stranger.

Except the stranger knew her name.

Putting the thought resolutely aside, she unlocked her dorm door. It was dark. Hard to tell if Margot was back and already asleep. She tiptoed across the room, trying not to make any noise.

She would have made it, too, except she stumbled.

She gave a little cry as she went down, grabbing at anything she could to keep her balance. She caught the edge of her desk chair and pulled it down with her. The chair must have hit the desk, because books fell, too.

Puzzled and annoyed, Danni groped for the light switch on the wall. But when her lamp came on, she saw that it had been knocked off the dresser, and lay on its side, casting an eerie glow across the floor.

Then she saw it.

Her gold sweater was on her bed, slashed to ribbons and splashed with red.

Danni turned away from the bed in horror, only to see something even more frightening.

On her mirror, in blood-red writing, was scrawled a horrible message: *YOU MUST DIE*.

Chapter 15

"Danni. What is it? What's wrong?" a voice said.

Danni wheeled around, her mouth open. Had she spoken? Had she cried out?

She realized she must have, for Mouse was standing in the door of the bathroom, wrapped in her demure chin-to-slippers bathrobe.

"Oh, Mouse, my God, look!" said Danni, pointing wildly at the mirror.

Mouse's lips moved soundlessly as she read the words on the mirror. Her face grew pale. "What does this mean?" she asked at last.

"Someone . . . hates me." Danni felt sick. The sweater looked as if it were bleeding from the slashes in it.

"Hey, dudettes!" Lacey's voice carolled from the next room. A moment later she stood in the bathroom doorway. "Mouse, tell me everything. What happ — "

The words froze on Lacey's lips. Then she said, "What *happened*?"

"I don't know," said Danni shakily. She righted her desk chair and sat down gingerly.

Lacey picked up the stabbed sweater.

"Be careful." Mouse's voice was urgent.

"It's okay. It's . . ." Lacey sniffed. "Nail polish. The stuff on the mirror looks like lipstick."

Danni said slowly, "That was the sweater Margot had borrowed. She just got it back from the cleaners yesterday."

"Who would have — " Mouse began.

"*Margot*," said Lacey.

"That's crazy," said Danni. "Really, really crazy."

There was a long silence, as Danni and Lacey remembered how Margot had freaked out about the sweater just a few days before.

At last, Lacey shrugged. "Well, someone else might have done this. Was the door locked?"

"I always lock the door," answered Danni.

"You know," Lacey said thoughtfully, "our door was unlocked."

Mouse paled. "What do you mean?"

"Just what I said. Our door was unlocked. So whoever did it could have come through our room."

"I would have heard them," declared Mouse.

Just then, Danni heard a sound — footsteps, softly and carefully, coming down the hallway. As if the person was creeping up slowly, trying to hear what was happening in room 2B before making herself known.

Danni knew who it was. It was her roommate.

Going to the door, Danni wondered how Margot would react when she heard what had happened. Would she give herself away? *Was* she the one to blame?

But when Danni looked out, no one was there. Danni heard a door click shut somewhere down the hallway. Other than that, the hall was quiet and empty.

"I thought I heard Margot," Danni said. "I guess not."

"Well," Lacey said after a moment, "we'd better go get Kendra."

"No!" said Danni.

Both Mouse and Lacey looked surprised. "Look," said Lacey, "we've got to report this."

"No," Danni repeated. "Let's just, let's just keep this quiet for now, okay?"

"*What!* Why?" demanded Lacey.

"I don't know. It's just a feeling I have."

"Danni, look, I know you're having a bad week here," Lacey began.

You don't know how bad, Danni thought.

"But it doesn't mean you can, you know, make it go away by ignoring it. This isn't some crank phone call. This is serious."

Mouse asked, "Do you think it's connected to the phone calls, Danni?"

"No!" cried Danni.

"Well, is anything missing, then?"

Danni scanned the room. "Not that I can tell, so far." Wearily she bent to pick up the lamp.

As Mouse helped Danni clean the terrifying message off her mirror, Lacey tried to direct everyone's attention away from what had happened. "How did your hot date go?"

It worked. Mouse was instantly diverted. "It wasn't a date," said Mouse. Then she smiled. "But it went fine."

"Did he say anything about another date?" asked Danni.

"No. But he gave me this." Mouse held up an envelope and, with a flourish, pulled out a folded sheet of paper. "I'm on. It's official. I'm on *The Chronicle*."

"Mouse, that's great! I can see it now, Maureen Rourke, News Editor, then Editor in Chief."

As Mouse began shaking her head, Danni said, "Lacey's right. You could be Editor in Chief. Why not?"

Mouse grinned. "Nah. Not News Editor, guys. *Sports* Editor."

She walked to the bathroom door and stopped. Over her shoulder she grinned. "I've always liked sports. I've always been pretty good at them."

Lacey and Danni stared after Mouse, open-mouthed.

Then Danni said, "Hey, Lacey."

"Hey what?"

"I think maybe you've created a monster . . ."

Chapter 16

It was late.

Mouse had gone to bed. Danni was changing into her nightshirt. She took off her sweater and opened the bottom drawer to shove it inside. Then she stopped.

"Margot," she whispered.

"Still unaccounted for," said Lacey. She yawned hugely. "Maybe I should check this library business out. There's obviously more to it than meets the eye."

"Margot's letter opener," whispered Danni, feeling the color drain from her face.

"What are you muttering about now?" said Lacey, exasperated. She walked over to where Danni was kneeling, both hands whiteknuckled as they clutched the edge of the drawer.

"The . . . letter opener. Margot's. My

sweater. Cut to shreds . . ." Danni felt her voice begin to rise hysterically.

"Chill. Okay?" Lacey squatted down beside Danni and peered in the drawer. There, nestled between two sweaters, was the ornate silver letter opener that belonged to Margot.

Lacey reached in and took it out. "Whoever left you the message must have put it in there."

"Margot?" Danni tried to speak calmly.

"Not necessarily. . . . anybody could have picked it up . . ."

"Hi, everybody, what's up?" Margot's voice interrupted Lacey.

The two girls turned.

Margot looked at them, and when she saw their expressions, her eyes widened. "What happened?"

Taking the letter opener gingerly from Lacey's hand, Danni walked toward Margot with it. "This is yours, I believe."

Margot drew back a little. Then she looked quickly around the room again. "Yeah. What are *you* doing with it?"

With a flourish, Lacey took the shredded sweater out of the plastic bag.

Margot gasped and recoiled. "Your sweater! Your beautiful sweater!"

"Yes," said Danni, staring hard at Margot. "I'm surprised you recognized it. I was barely able to, and it's *my* sweater."

"What do you mean?" Again giving Danni no chance to answer, Margot rushed on. "Who did this? And why?" she cried.

"I don't know," said Danni. "And you should have seen the lovely message someone left on the mirror: 'You must die.' "

"Oh, Danni, do you think it has anything to do with the phone calls?"

"Funny you should ask that," said Danni.

"And I didn't — I thought maybe it was some kind of joke you were pulling. Oh, Danni, I'm *sorry*." Margot walked over and gave Danni a hug. "Will you forgive me?" she whispered in her ear.

"Touching," commented Lacey dryly. She yawned again. "Look, somebody's got an enemy here. If you won't report it, then you're going to have to be careful. Extra careful."

Danni nodded slowly. "I know."

"What do you mean?" asked Margot.

Danni looked at her roommate. "Because someone is after me," she said flatly. "Someone is going to get me if I don't watch out."

* * *

Danni opened her mailbox and made a face. Nothing.

"Like, have you ever thought when you put your hand in the mailbox what might be waiting in there?" a voice said at her shoulder.

"I was hoping to shake hands with some mail, Jordan," said Danni without turning around. "Have you been following me?"

"How did you know it was me?" asked Jordan, half-pleased, half-chagrined.

"Easy," said Danni. "Only you could turn a trip to the post office into a potential horror story."

"Want to avoid the horror story of dinner at Salem and go get something to eat?"

"Thanks," said Danni. "But I can't."

Jordan's eyes darkened. "Can't? Or won't? Are you still mad at me about the other night?"

"The other night?" Danni was startled. For a moment, she thought he meant what she'd found in her room. Then she realized he was talking about the practical joke in the topiary garden. "Oh, that. No. Apology accepted."

"Then why won't you go get some dinner with me? Everybody's got to eat." Jordan put his arm possessively around Danni's shoulder.

"Jordan, I can't. I've got too much to do.

Really." As casually as she could, Danni slid out from under Jordan's arm. "Listen, call me. We'll make some plans."

"Tonight," said Jordan.

"Okay," said Danni. She turned and walked out of the post office and back in the direction of her dorm. She could feel Jordan's eyes on her as she left.

The feeling of being watched stayed with her all the way back to the dorm. She couldn't help looking over her shoulder. Once, she thought she saw someone duck out of sight behind one of the big oaks near the far end of the walk. But it seemed so ridiculous. Other students were hurrying across campus, and no one seemed to notice anything. Surely if someone was following her, lurching and ducking from tree to tree, it wouldn't go unnoticed.

Paranoid, you're getting paranoid, she told herself. No one is following you. Why would they be? Stop it!

Forcing herself to turn around and not look back again, Danni headed to her dorm room.

But even back in the dorm room, she couldn't sit still. She pulled the curtains shut, turned on the lights. The ugly remnants of her sweater had gone in the garbage. The ugly words were gone from the mirror. She should try and forget. Think about something else.

She realized she hadn't eaten since breakfast.

"That's what it is," she told herself. She got up and called through the bathroom, "Lacey? Mouse? Anybody home?"

No one answered. For a moment, she considered going back out to grab something at the Student Center. But it was getting late.

She didn't want to eat in the Quad caf alone. It made her feel left out and lonely, and she didn't know enough people yet to be sure of running into someone to sit with.

That left the Dungeon vending machines.

Rummaging around, she came up with a handful of change and headed downstairs.

The Dungeon was jumping. Two girls she didn't recognize passed, jogging in bike shorts and sweaty tank tops, their faces red. The sound of television blasted from the lounge. Further down the hall, three girls were sitting on the uncomfortable orange vinyl sofas outside the laundry room, quizzing each other. How could they concentrate with all the noise? Danni wondered.

She reached the vending machines and smiled at an extremely skinny girl who had just cranked out four Mars bars.

"The four food groups, right?" Danni asked.

The girl rolled her eyes and walked away without answering.

"Excuuuuuse me," muttered Danni. She fished in her pocket and came up with the change. She bought a bag of M&M's and another bag of taco chips. She tipped the M&M's into the taco chips and began to eat them mixed together as she wandered out into the Dungeon.

She had never walked all the way through the basement before. She decided that now was as good time as any.

It *was* huge. An exercise group of some sort was finishing up in an enormous room just past one of the turns. She found out that there were laundry rooms under four dorms. The joggers passed her three more times as she walked. She discovered side halls with smaller rooms opening off them, mini-study lounges, apparently. Some had been claimed. In one, a girl, her glasses precariously askew on her nose, had fallen asleep with a chem book open across her chest.

Danni remembered her first reaction to the Dungeon. The feeling of claustrophobia, of being trapped. Well, it *was* pretty institutional. But now it seemed friendly, casual.

She smiled at the joggers. This part of the Dungeon was beneath her dorm, wasn't it?

Or was it? Oh well, she could ask someone.

She turned down one of the side halls, looking for a studious person. But all the little rooms were empty.

Stepping back out, she looked up and down the hall. Empty.

Like one of those horror films, she thought. Where the hero wakes up one morning and her whole town is missing.

Stop that, she scolded herself.

From far away, she heard the sound of voices. She started walking toward them.

And then she had the feeling again. That feeling of being watched. Of being followed.

She looked over her shoulder. Nothing. Just a long expanse of empty hall.

So empty.

Involuntarily, she picked up the pace.

The lights flickered.

She began to run.

There. Wasn't that the door? She ran faster, clutching the empty, balled up taco chips bag in her hand. Faster.

Faster.

A door swung open.

Danni screamed as a figure leaped out.

Chapter 17

The girl screamed, too, dropping a load of laundry so it spilled out onto the floor at Danni's feet.

Danni clapped her hand over her own mouth.

The girl stopped screaming and stared at Danni. "What — what is it?" she gasped. She looked past Danni down the hall.

Danni could tell by the girl's face that no one — no monster, no crazy person — was behind her.

"Nothing!" She'd never felt so stupid in her whole life. At least the girl wasn't someone she knew. What if it had been someone like Jodie? The whole dorm would have known in no time that Danni had been lurking in the Dungeon, screaming and acting crazy. Aloud, Danni said, "I was just in a hurry and you startled me, that's all. Here, let me help you pick that up."

"Are you sure? I mean, are you sure you're

okay? You look kind of pale," the girl said.

"I'm surprised I'm not turning red with embarrassment," said Danni, bending and scooping the clothes back in the basket, and helping the girl pick it up. "I'm sorry I scared you."

"Hey, no problem," said the girl. She hoisted the basket to her hip, and hurried down the hall. At the corner she looked back.

Danni waved weakly.

She was alone again in the hall.

She didn't stop to look around this time, but ran all the way back up to her room.

"Lacey!"

Lacey was annoyed. "I'm trying to concentrate on this, okay, Mouse? Like, there's a test or something tomorrow, I think."

"Lacey!"

"What?" Lacey looked up to see Mouse backing out of the bathroom, both hands over her mouth.

"Mouse, what is it? What's wrong?" Lacey dropped her book and jumped up to grab Mouse by the elbow.

Her roommate's face was ghostly underneath the makeup she'd just gone into the bathroom to wash off. Her eyes were dilated with shock like a frightened animal's.

"Mouse?" Lacey shook Mouse's arm. "What is it? Answer me!"

"The bathroom. The mirror. In the bathroom."

"What, you broke it? Great, seven years bad luck . . ." Lacey let go of Mouse's arm and thrust open the bathroom door. "My God, not again . . ."

The silvery surface was streaked with red. For one awful, heartstopping moment Lacey thought of ax-murderers and serial killers and looked wildly around the tiny bathroom. But no body was tucked between the toilet and the wall. No gruesome corpse was curled around the wastebasket under the tiny sink.

The only casualty was a virtually decapitated lipstick in the sink. As Lacey looked dumbly down at it, she realized that once again, the bloody mess on the mirror was lipstick. A little more calmly, she surveyed the lurid slashes on the glass.

This time bloody red letters spelled out, *YOU'LL BE PUNISHED*.

Lacey closed her eyes and opened them again. The words were still there. Quickly she reached out and opened the door to the other room.

Danni was lying motionless, face down on the bed.

Chapter 18

"Oh, no!" gasped Lacey. "No! Danni, Danni!" She leaped across the room just as Danni rolled over, her eyes fluttering open.

"Arrgh!" cried Lacey, stumbling back.

Yawning, Danni sat up. She rubbed her eyes. "Lacey? Wow, I must have sacked. What time is it?"

"How long have you been in here?" Lacey demanded.

Still sleepy, Danni said, "I don't know. An hour maybe?"

"Have you been in the bathroom?"

"No." Danni hesitated, then said, "I went down to the basement for some candy. I ran back up here and sort of lay down for a minute. I guess I was more tired than I realized, or something."

Danni's gaze sharpened as she took in Lacey's frightened face. "Why? What's wrong?"

"You'd better come look," said Lacey grimly.

Danni followed Lacey into the bathroom.

Lacey stepped aside and Danni faced her own reflection in the mirror: her reflection, slashed again and again with red.

She tried to speak. But the red filled her vision. The red of blood. The red of death.

Then Danni began to shake her head. "No," she whispered. "No."

"It's not my lipstick," said Lacey, pointing to the smeared golden tube in the sink, "and I know it's not Mouse's. She doesn't wear lipstick. Her mouth's all wrong for it."

Danni looked down into the sink. She moaned softly. "It's mine," said Danni. "It's mine."

Her eyes met Lacey's in the mirror.

"What am I going to do?" she implored Lacey. "Tell me what to do!"

"We've got to tell Kendra."

"No!"

"Danni. . . . this affects all of us."

"But it was meant for me! I know it was."

"How do you know, Danni? This could be meant for any of us. We've *got* to tell Kendra."

"No! No, I know it's me," said Danni desperately.

Mouse had come into the bathroom and was staring at the red letters as if mesmerized. "This could be meant for any of us. Some creep, some sicko. . . ."

"No," said Danni. "No, it's for me."

She had started to shake. She was trembling so much she could barely speak. She opened her mouth but no words came out.

Then she whispered at last, "I know it's for me. Because it's the same as the calls. The phone calls. Those were the exact words."

When Margot came in that night, Danni pretended to be asleep. She watched her roommate getting ready for bed through her eyelashes. It couldn't be Margot doing all those things. Could it?

Margot had been a little distant at first, but they'd become friends. Close friends. Margot seemed to really like her, to enjoy hanging out with her. She was always asking Danni's advice. Even imitating some of the things Danni did — subconsciously, of course. Besides, imitation was the sincerest form of flattery.

Of course, Margot could be a sort of cold. A bit reserved. Almost secretive. Danni frowned. What sort of secret was Margot keeping? Surely nothing terrible. Nothing like, I'm an ax-murderer and you're next, roommate.

No. Besides, what had she ever done to Margot, except be her friend?

I'm going crazy, Danni thought. It can't be Margot. It just can't be.

But who else could it be?

Mouse?

No way.

But wait a minute. Mouse wasn't as meek as she seemed. She'd undergone a startling transformation with help from Lacey. Maybe Mouse had one of those split personalities — like Dr. Jekyll and Mr. Hyde. Mouse could have made the phone calls. There was a pay phone at the end of the hall. She could have run down there and made the first call, for example, then come back and pretended she'd been asleep and hadn't heard the phone ring. She could have shredded the sweater, too, and not really been asleep at all. Maybe she'd just been in there waiting, waiting for Danni to come home. . . .

And it would have been easy to write on the mirror, then pretend to Lacey that she'd just discovered it.

But why? It didn't make any sense.

Of course, if you were some kind of psychopath, it didn't have to make sense. After all, what did she or anyone really know about Mouse? Just that she'd led an incredibly sheltered life. That she talked to her parents every Sunday afternoon. That she was shy, but not too shy to try out for the school paper *and* the cute guy who worked there.

That she knew a lot about psychology because her parents were shrinks.

At least, that's what she said. But maybe they weren't shrinks at all. Maybe Mouse knew all about abnormal psychology because *she* was abnormal. Crazy.

Maybe behind that mousey exterior, there beat the heart of a maniac.

Mouse? *Mouse??*

Impossible.

Putting the thought of Mouse out of her mind, Danni turned her attention to Lacey.

Lacey the attention junkie. Lacey loved excitement. She liked a thrill. Was this sort of thing exciting to her? Tormenting someone, playing horrible jokes on them?

She'd freely admitted she was considered the juvenile delinquent in her family. A bad little girl. The black sheep daughter.

But Lacey would never cut up a cashmere sweater, thought Danni. Never.

Would she?

If she was bored enough, she might. Who knows? Maybe that would seem exciting to her.

And she could have made the phone calls. She could have gotten home before Mouse and written on the mirror.

But why?

A psycho's idea of fun.

And maybe that's why Lacey kept on insisting she was different. Maybe when she described herself as crazy, wild, *she really meant it*.

Maybe she was trying to tell Danni, tell them all something. Trying to warn them.

But why is she picking on me? wondered Danni, thinking how casually cruel, how devastatingly ruthless Lacey could be. She shivered inwardly.

And then, randomly, her thoughts leaped to Jordan. In a way, he was the best candidate of all. That husky whisper on the phone could easily have been his voice.

But it would have been almost impossible for him to get into her room and tear up her sweater. Impossible, too, to get in to write on the mirror.

No. Not Jordan.

Margot had finished getting ready for bed. She got in, reached up for the light. Looked over at Danni.

Danni forced herself to stay absolutely still, breathing deeply.

Margot's face was expressionless. At last she reached up and turned off the light.

And the dark closed over Danni's head.

Chapter 19

The sun woke Danni the next morning. For a moment, she forgot everything that had happened the night before. For a moment, she smiled: a golden autumn day with only one class, and then the freedom to do whatever she wanted. Maybe Margot wanted to go shopping. Maybe Mouse needed some more clothes for her new look. . . .

Then the joy went out of the day as she remembered what had happened.

Trapped, she thought, rolling heavily over to sit up. I'm trapped.

She looked over at Margot's side of the room. The bed was neatly made. A stack of books stood on her desk, another beside her bed. Her bathrobe hung on the back of the door.

The letter opener lay on top of the chest of drawers.

Trapped. The word echoed in her head.

The bell tolled.

The day was beginning.

With the weary shuffle of a prisoner, Danni got out of bed and began to get ready for classes.

On the terrace of the Student Center, Lacey sat brooding, holding a cup of coffee in her hands. She should be in class, but she couldn't get interested in it. She was annoyed with herself. She was letting things get to her. And when you let things get to you, you could lose control.

A familiar figure caught her eye.

Danni.

She was walking slowly, staring down in front of her, her books hugged to her chest. Positively, thought Lacey, a Mouse-like pose.

Or the pose of the *former* Mouse. Now Mouse walked more confidently, smiled more easily.

It was almost as if Danni and Mouse had changed places.

Lacey watched Danni until she disappeared from sight. It couldn't be easy, what Danni was going through. She tried to imagine what Danni must be feeling. Did she think someone was watching her? Following her? Waiting until she got home to call up and whisper threats into the telephone?

Did she wonder who it could be? Did Danni suspect anyone?

Did she suspect the truth?

Or had she been pushed so far to the edge that she couldn't think at all?

A hand touched her shoulder lightly.

"Lacey?"

Lacey turned and smiled. It was a smile no one at Salem College would recognize. Warm. Friendly. Earnest. Sincere.

"Jordan," she said softly. "Jordan, we've got to talk."

Jordan looked uneasy. "Here? Now? Do you think — "

Lacey cut him off. "It's important, Jordan. Very, very important." She lowered her voice even more. "It's about Danni."

"Maureen," said Pete, "have you heard *anything* I said?"

Mouse looked up. The two of them were in *The Chronicle* office. They'd been there ever since lunch. The afternoon was beginning to wane.

Mouse was proofreading a piece she'd just

finished about crime on campus. But her mind wasn't on it.

"Maureen?"

Her eyes focused on Pete. What would he think if he knew the truth?

And would she ever have the courage to tell him?

But in a way, she was living a lie. And there had been too many lies, too many twisted, terrible lies already. It had gotten out of hand.

She took a big breath. What was the best place to start? Maybe by confession of the littlest of the lies.

"Pete," she said, with a sigh. "I've got something to tell you."

Pete reached out and took her hand. He smiled at her warmly and she felt tears sting her eyes. "Oh, Pete . . ."

This has been the longest day of my life, thought Margot as she cut across the Commons by the Student Center. She hadn't heard a word in any of her classes. Instead, she'd found herself thinking about her roommates. About everything that had happened.

About her life.

If you can call it a life, she thought grimly.

It was ironic, really, when you thought about it.

The bitter rage, the hatred that had been her companion for almost as long as she could remember welled up inside her. I wish they were all dead, she thought. I could kill them all.

It's not my fault.

I couldn't help it.

Could I?

But maybe she could. Maybe it was just a matter of self-discipline, like everything else. Maybe that was where she'd failed.

Failed.

Failed.

Long shadows were beginning to creep from beneath the pin oaks to merge with the dusk. The darkness fell on her like a weight she could never shake off.

She'd thought she could do it. She'd almost pulled it off.

But she'd failed.

Suddenly up ahead, far up ahead, she saw a figure hurrying through the thickening shadows.

Danni. Was it?

Almost unconsciously, Margot's pace quickened. Maybe she hadn't failed after all. After all, it wasn't over.

Not yet.

Danni walked briskly, head held high. She was telling herself what an ordinary day it had been. Classes. Lunch at the Student Center. A quick conversation with Jordan. She'd been hoping he'd ask her out for the weekend, but he hadn't.

On the other hand, he'd said he'd call her.

She'd almost said, If I'm still alive.

But she hadn't.

By the light of day, her fears had gradually melted. She realized she'd been exaggerating. The thing to do was to confront her fears.

She'd decided she'd get her roommates together and talk the whole thing over, honestly and openly. See what they knew. See what they suspected.

And she'd felt better. She could handle this. She could.

She'd been thinking about it all so hard that she'd forgotten to think about the sense that she was being followed.

Not until she reached the walk leading to the Quad did the feeling catch up with her.

Then she realized it. It was with her now.

It had been with her all day. That feeling of being followed. That feeling of being watched.

Her chin lifted. She forced herself not to look back. She knew it wouldn't do any good.

She forced herself not to run.

Let whoever it was see that she wasn't afraid. She wasn't going to give up. She'd fight whoever it was.

Fight them to the death.

Quad Main loomed up out of the gathering darkness like a leering jack-o'-lantern. But its ghoulish appearance was belied by the crowds of students going in and out, laughing and talking, or walking close to one another, talking seriously. It was belied, too, by the smell of cooking that came from the Quad cafeteria, by the faint sounds of life that came through the windows, some of which were still open, a little, in spite of the brisk fall air. Music from radios and CD players, of telephones ringing and doors closing, and showers running, of more laughter, and even the sound of somebody singing happily off key. And if someone looked behind the windows, opened them like the windows on an advent calendar, they would see all the scenes of normal life: people talking, people arguing, people reading, people studying, people polishing fingernails and toenails, working on computers, sleeping, dreaming.

"I'm home," said Danni defiantly to the empty room. No one answered her. No one was in suite 2AB.

Danni shrugged. It was just as well. She'd grab a shower, wash some of the worry and grubbiness of the day off. Make herself a little more human.

A few minutes later, Danni pushed open the door to the showers. The room was empty, a long, gleaming rectangular box of shining tile and polished chrome, silent except for the drip, drip, drip of a faucet.

Good. She had it all to herself.

She went to the last stall, where the hot water was best, and turned it on full blast. Slipping out of her robe, she stepped gratefully into the shower.

She was almost finished when the lights flickered and went out, plunging her into total darkness.

Chapter 20

It was worse than any nightmare. For one horrible moment she stood in the hot water, trying to see, trying to understand what had happened. Then, her hands trembling violently, she reached out and fumbled with the knobs.

It was a miracle she didn't scald herself to death.

But at last they were turned off.

The darkness was absolute.

But the silence was not.

From not so far away, she could hear shrieks.

The sound panicked her. She banged into the wall of the shower, turned, and hit the edge of one of the faucets. The pain forced her to stop, to get a grip. Thrusting her hands out, she began to grope her way out of the dark stall.

After what seemed like an eternity, she found her robe and put it on. Painstakingly she began to feel her way out along the wall.

Where was she? In the dark, she was completely turned around.

Until the door opened almost on top of her.

Danni screamed. The screams echoed off the tile, reverberated out into the hall.

And the lights came on.

Kendra, holding a flashlight, clicked it off and grabbed Danni by the arm and gave her a quick shake.

"Hold on to it, kiddo, we just had a power outage, that's all."

"A power outage?"

"The wiring in these dorms is pretty old stuff. Sometimes it gets balky." Kendra made a face. "Probably something to do with whatever they're cooking in the caf. Nothing to worry about. The power outages, I mean, not the food in the caf."

"Oh." Danni smiled weakly.

"You okay?"

Danni nodded, feeling foolish. "I'm fine," she assured Kendra.

"Good."

Kendra bustled away, leaving Danni to

gather up her shower gear and head shakily back to her room.

"Whew," she said aloud.

She pulled on a pair of jeans and a sweatshirt. The lights flickered and Danni froze. But they stayed on.

"Hi!" Margot bounded through the door. "Where is everybody?"

"*I'm* here," said Danni, pretending to be insulted. Seeing Margot, who looked so cheerful and normal, Danni could almost forget her suspicions, her fears.

"How 'bout that lights out," Margot went on. "Pretty radical, huh? I'm going to carry a flashlight from now on!"

"Radically scary," said Danni. "I was in the shower!"

Margot made a face. "Creepy. Like a Hitchcock movie, or something."

"Or something," agreed Danni. "What's happening?"

"I'm going to the basement to do the study thing. While watching TV of course." Margot laughed. "You learn twice as much when you study and watch TV, right?"

"Absolutely."

"Want to come join me?"

Danni hesitated. "I don't know."

"Oh, c'mon. Listen, I'll head down, raid the vending machines, and meet you in the lounge." Margot ripped a sheet of paper out of her notebook, scribbled on it, and disappeared into the next room. Returning, she explained, "I told Lacey and Mouse where we'd be. Maybe they'll come down, too."

"I don't know," Danni repeated.

Margot looked surprised. "No big deal. If you feel like it, you know where to find me."

She grabbed up her notebook and a handful of change, and bounded out of the room.

Margot the manic, thought Danni. Probably the tension. It's probably getting to all of us.

She looked around the empty room. Why not? Why not join Margot and pig out and watch TV until her brain was fried?

Danni walked down the last flight of stairs. She pushed open the door and stepped out into the basement hall, half expecting to see a girl with a load of laundry charging at her. But it was quiet. People had probably deserted the Dungeon when the lights had gone out.

She walked slowly down the hall. It was silent all around her. Faintly, she heard the sound of the TV in the lounge. She walked toward it.

The TV in the lounge was on. But no one was there.

Danni stepped into the lounge. She put her hand up on the wall.

"Margot?" she called softly.

She heard a sound behind her.

And the lights went out again.

This time Danni didn't scream. Something kept her quiet. As quiet as the basement.

As quiet as Margot.

She stayed still. So still. So still for so long that the violent pounding of her heart slowed down to a dull, terrified *thud thud*.

So still she could hear the sound of the water flowing through the pipes overhead.

So still that she heard the whisper of a footstep right behind her.

She still didn't scream. Instead she turned, flicking the flashlight on.

Light glinted on metal. One horrible scream reverberated down the tunnel.

The flashlight was knocked out of her hand.

She scrambled for it on her hands and knees, heedless of her palms tearing against the concrete floor.

There. There, she had it. She was safe, now.

She turned the flashlight off and moved away from where she'd found it, as quickly and quietly as possible. The light could show her the way out.

But it also made her a target.

As silently, as stealthily as she could, she inched forward, her hand outstretched, hoping for a wall. Fearing human flesh.

When her hand touched the wall, the cold unexpectedness of it made her jump. The flashlight almost slipped from her sweating hand. But she caught it.

She began to edge along the wall, straining to see in the absolute darkness of the Dungeon, trying to imagine where she was.

And trying not to imagine what was waiting for her.

The knife. A great, glittering scimitar of a knife. And a hand.

She inched along the wall and came to a door frame. The basement stairs?

She risked the quick flick of the light. No. A study room. Empty.

Afraid of who — or what — might have seen her in the creeping darkness, she dropped down and made herself walk as quickly and silently as possible to the far wall.

And touched something soft.

And living.

Something that grabbed onto her arm.

Without thinking she jerked back, raising the flashlight and turning it on.

It wasn't who she'd expected to see.

"Lacey," she gasped.

A horrible scream rang out and the knife flashed down again.

Chapter 21

The flashlight fell from her nerveless fingers. It rolled a few feet, spinning horrible, distorted images with its light.

And then the flashlight went out.

It had all happened so fast that she almost didn't believe it.

Didn't believe that she was trapped in the basement with a madwoman.

Didn't believe she was going to die.

Heedless now of noise, she began to run, her arms stretched out in front of her.

She banged into a wall. Fell. Scrambled to her feet. The sound of her breathing filled her ears. She tried to stop, to hold her breath, anything not to make so much noise.

But it was useless.

She was going to die.

Still she struggled. A wall, a door. A chair.

Her palms were bloody, her shins bruised.

She almost welcomed the pain. At least it meant she was still alive.

She blundered on, expecting every moment to hear the whisper of the knife coming down.

Hearing instead, from what direction she didn't know, the deadly whisper of her name.

"No," she whimpered, before she could stop herself.

The whisper stopped.

She'd given herself away.

She leaped forward, hands scrabbling madly. What did it feel like, the knife? Would it hurt? Would she keep trying to run, keep trying to get up?

Behind her.

No.

She turned. Ducked. Stumbled forward.

And ahead of her, an alarm went off as a door opened.

A square of light appeared.

The emergency exit.

She ran toward it with all her might, never thinking who might have opened it, never thinking it might be a trap.

Never thinking how she might be silhouetted against the light, an easy target.

Until Danni stepped into the doorway in front of her.

Margot swerved. Ducked. Crashed against the wall as the blade came down, just missing her.

She rolled to her knees. "Danni," she cried. "Danni, don't!"

Danni stopped, the knife raised.

"Why?" asked Margot hoarsely. "*Why*, Danni?"

Was Danni surprised by the question? It was hard to tell, hard to see her face in the light from the door. But the blade flashed as her hand wavered.

"Danni, *please*."

"No," said Danni. "You can't trick me. You're against me! You're all against me. But I'm special."

"You are," said Margot. "You are, Danni. When I first saw you, I knew you were special."

"Yes," said Danni in a voice that was falsely pleasant. "They've always told me I was special. That's why I had my own wing in the house. And someone to stay with me all the time. They told me I was special. And I knew I was. But they didn't really mean what they told me."

"Why not?" asked Margot. The words were a ghastly silver thread, holding the knife above her head, preventing it from coming down.

"Because they were *stupid*." Danni's voice hardened. "And they *lied* to me. But I fooled them. I found out about college and real life. I found out that special people didn't have to live alone with a companion who was paid to watch you."

"What did you do?"

"I killed her," said Danni simply. "And I escaped. I planned and planned. Wrote letters. It was so easy."

"And you came here. To Salem."

"Yes. No one knew. No one guessed. But *you*. You started making fun of me. Started copying me."

"Danni, no. I *admired* you. I knew you were special . . ." Margot's voice broke off.

"You're lying. You guessed about me. You were going to send me back!" cried Danni. "You're just like all the rest of them. And you will be PUNISHED!"

"Margot! Look out!" Mouse's voice from behind Danni startled her. She hesitated.

With one last desperate lunge, Margot sprinted forward.

And then suddenly, uniforms were all

around her. Cops. Security guards. Danni's screams rolled down the dark hallways, mingled with the cries and warnings of the police.

Margot fell into Mouse's arms, trying not to hear Danni's mad voice behind her.

"NOOOO, NOOOOO. Let me go, I'll kill you, I'll kill you, you can't do this to me . . . NOOOOOO."

"L-Lacey," gasped Margot. "Oh, Lacey."

"Hey, it's cool," said a familiar voice. The two girls looked up to see Lacey, one hand closed into a fist, edging around the mass of cops.

"Your hand," cried Mouse.

"She just nicked my palm a little. That oughtta make telling my fortune special," Lacey joked.

"How can you joke at a time like this?" asked Mouse.

The three of them retreated out the door and stepped back as four security guards began to lead Danni out of the Dungeon.

It was a Danni none of them recognized, her eyes wild, her voice hoarse, her hair a demonic tangled halo around her head.

"No," she was panting. "No. Noooo."

Her strength seemed almost inhuman, but they held on. Behind them, another cop was picking up the knife carefully, so he wouldn't leave fingerprints.

They watched silently as their roommate was led away. As she passed them, she stopped struggling for a moment.

Margot's eyes met Danni's. For a moment, the Danni she remembered at her best looked back. Then the eyes gleamed red and crazy. "You," spat Danni. "It's all your fault. You'll pay for this. I'll get you for this . . ." Her voice rose in a shriek and then someone dragged her hands behind her back and cuffed her and they began to take her to the waiting car.

"How can I joke at a time like this, Mouse?" asked Lacey. She looked at the car, now pulling away, the lights flashing. "What else can I do?" She turned her head away and her voice was harsh. "Cry?"

Chapter 22

A few hours later the three roommates were sprawled around Suite 2AB. "So I kind of suspected something was up," Lacey was explaining, "but I couldn't put my finger on it. I kept hoping Mouse, with all her training in psych, would figure it out."

"It's one thing to read about crazy people," said Mouse soberly. "It's another to actually be around one."

"She didn't act crazy," said Margot. "At least not at first. She seemed so normal. So nice."

Lacey shook her head. "One thing Danni wasn't, was normal."

Margot shuddered. "What about the phone calls?"

"They were all in her head. You didn't hear the phone ring that night she said she got the first call, Mouse. Remember?"

"And we weren't home the second time it happened," Mouse said.

"Yes. But *she* believed them. I think Danni started to sense that she wasn't quite pulling it off. That someone was onto her. And she'd already murdered her nurse, so she knew she was guilty. She was losing her grip on reality and all she could think was to protect herself. But not in any logical way. She wasn't thinking like a logical, normal person.

"For some reason, she fixated on you, Margot. She thought you'd stolen her sweater, put your letter opener in her drawer. I think she really believed you were after her."

"Danni shredded the sweater and wrote on the mirror herself, didn't she?" asked Margot.

"Yes," Lacey said. "She was really crazy."

Mouse was shaking her head. "But how did you know, Lacey?"

"I didn't, exactly. But things just kept not adding up. For example, I noticed that all — and I do mean *all* — of Danni's clothes were *brand new*. And that she paid for everything in cash, like she didn't want to be traced. And she never got any mail, although she made a big deal about going to the mailbox, or talking about calling her family. So when we got our phone bills, I sort of checked hers out. There were *no* long distance phone calls on it."

"Wow," said Mouse. "That's good, Lacey."

Margot said thoughtfully. "Yeah, it is. But I never could believe something was wrong. I knew my letter opener wasn't sharp enough to rip up a sweater like that. But that's what Danni was trying to make it look like, wasn't it? She hated me so much. She told me — down there in the Dungeon — that she thought some of the things I did were to make fun of her. And that I was doing that because I'd caught on to her. But I hadn't. Yet."

"But *you* had, Lacey," said Mouse.

Lacey shrugged. "Not entirely. I was suspicious. But not that she was a psycho-killer. I just thought she was a little crazy. So I started keeping an eye on her. And discovered she was doing the same to you, Margot."

"Ugh." Margot shuddered.

"So then I decided to have a little talk with Jordan. I thought maybe he could give me a little perspective. He'd started wondering, too. By then, of course, Danni was really starting to lose it. Imitating normal was getting to be too much for her."

"You're lucky to be alive, Margot," Lacey went on. "After all, you wouldn't have been the first person she'd killed."

The three roommates were silent, then, thinking about what the police had told them.

According to her parents — who were indeed very, very wealthy — Danni had always been a strange child. But as she got older she'd become more and more violent and paranoid, until, by the time she was seven or eight, she had to be watched all the time. Gradually one wing of the enormous house in which she lived had become a sort of posh prison for the increasingly psychotic child, with bars on the windows and paid companions and nurses twenty-four hours a day.

But Danni had, in her own dark way, dreamed of a normal life. She had secretly managed to get an application for Salem and, when her parents had left in the fall for their usual extended tour of remote places, she had made her escape, killing the companion who was in charge of her at the time. The woman had been stabbed to death with a knife.

"She brought the knife here . . . No one knew where she'd gone. They couldn't find her parents. And the family is so rich and well-connected that it was kept quiet," said Lacey.

"Maybe it was your letter opener that did it," suggested Mouse to Margot. "Maybe that's why she sort of fixated on you."

Margot shook her head. "I still can't believe it. I mean, when she made that fuss about the sweater, I was upset, but I thought maybe I was overreacting."

"You should learn to trust yourself," said Lacey.

"And you should learn to trust other people," Mouse told Lacey. "That goes for you, too, Lacey."

"I don't know what you're talking about," said Lacey.

"I mean, you've been pretending you're just a dumb party animal the whole time you've been here. That's all we've heard. But you're not. You didn't figure all of this out by being stupid, did you?"

Lacey looked sheepish. "Well, no."

"Just out of curiosity, Lacey, what kind of grades did you make in high school?"

For the first time since they'd been at Salem, Margot and Mouse saw the indomitable Lacey blush. "Straight A's," she confessed. "But I *hate* being labelled smart. I hate labels."

"Then why work so hard to be labelled an airhead? Why not be yourself?" asked Mouse.

"Like you?" said Lacey defensively.

But Mouse had changed. "You brought out some good things in me, Lacey. I like a lot about the new me. But I told Pete the truth, too. And I told him he could call me Mouse. That's me, too."

"After all that work!" said Lacey in mock indignation. But she was smiling.

Mouse turned to Margot, who held up her hands. "What is this supposed to be, truth or dare?"

"Your turn," chortled Lacey. "Truth."

"I think you already figured some of it out, Lacey," said Margot. She took a deep breath. "I'm a scholarship student. The rest of my stuff hasn't arrived because there isn't any more. I don't have pictures of my family because my mother and father died when I was a little girl. I've been raised by foster parents ever since. I hated where I'd come from. One of the reasons, I think, that Danni started not to trust me was because, in a way, she recognized what I was doing: I was watching her, using her as a role model for how to act, what to wear. She even caught me sleeping in her bed once. I didn't mean to, but I fell asleep, lying there, trying to imagine what it would be like to be 'normal' like Danni, believe it or not. Boy, was I wrong about that.

"I didn't want anybody to know how different I was. I didn't want anyone to know where

I'd come from. I didn't want them to hold it against me."

"Oh, Margot, how could we?" asked Mouse. "I like *you*. For you."

"Yeah, Margot, you're all right," agreed Lacey nonchalantly.

"Lacey, you overwhelm me," said Margot, smiling a little. "Anyway, you two must like me. You saved my life."

"All I did was go for help, like Lacey told me," Mouse said. "She's the one who saw your note and got worried about you."

"But why?" asked Margot. "Why then?"

Lacey said, "I'd done a little snooping in Danni's things earlier. And I'd found the knife. The *real* knife. The mother of all butcher knives. Then, when I saw your note, for some reason I looked to see if the knife was still there. It wasn't. That's when I got worried."

"Oh, God," said Margot. "I didn't know what was going on. I just knew that someone was after me with a knife."

"Well, it's over now." Lacey yawned hugely. "I'm going to take a little nap. About a twenty-four-hour one."

"I'm going to bed, too," said Mouse. "What about you, Margot?"

Margot looked down at her skinned palms

and dirty jeans and shirt. "I think I'm going to take a shower first. I'm a mess."

"Well, g'night," said Lacey.

" 'Night, roommates," said Margot.

The shower room was empty at that time of the night. Hardly surprising, thought Margot. She made her way slowly down the row of showers. She needed a shower badly. She needed to wash off all the fear and anger and exhaustion. And then she was going to take the world's longest nap.

She turned on the water. Steam billowed up around her. The shower at the end definitely had the best hot water.

Carefully she put her shower gear down on the ledge inside the shower. She stripped off her robe and stepped inside.

It felt great. After a few minutes she began to relax, making herself as mindless as the water that poured down on her.

She didn't know how long she'd been there before she sensed that she wasn't alone.

"Hello?" she called.

No one answered.

Frowning, Margot turned off the shower to listen. "Hello?" she said again.

Her voice echoed hollowly around the empty room.

Shaking her head at her stupid nerves she turned the shower back on and lifted her face to the water.

That's when she saw it out of the corner of her eye. A shadowy figure just beyond the shower curtain.

She opened her mouth to scream and choked on the water. She gasped and spluttered as the figure raised its arm.

"No," she gasped. "No!"

She grabbed the shower curtain instinctively, shrinking back against the wall.

And saw Lacey.

"Margot? What's the matter? It's just me." Lacey held up a silver bottle. "Listen, I thought you might like some of this bath gel goo. It feels great and it's good for sore muscles."

"Oh. Yeah. Gee, thanks, Lacey."

"No problem." Lacey grinned over her shoulder as she turned to leave. "Hey. You weren't scared, were you, Margot?"

"Me? Nah," said Margot. "Not me. I knew it was you the whole time. I wasn't scared. I wasn't scared at all."

Return to Nightmare Hall . . .
if you dare.

Deadly Attraction

Each time Hailey watched the scene play in slow motion in her mind, her stomach would churn and her pulse would race and her heart would begin thudding violently in her chest.

Because she knew what was coming.

She would close her eyes and try to stop it, try to make it end, but it wouldn't.

It would play on . . .

She was at Burgers Etc. It was the night Darlene Riggs and Robert Q Parker, III, first met. Tray in hand, Darlene glided slowly around the room in her black shorts and white T-shirt, slowly, so slowly. Robert Q's head turned, bit by bit, following her every move and the line of her body.

It should have been a night like any other.

But it wasn't. Because it had been the beginning . . .

The beginning of all the horror.

About the Author

"Writing tales of horror makes it hard to convince people that I'm a nice, gentle person," says **Diane Hoh.**

"So what's a nice woman like me doing scaring people?

"Having the time of my life. Discovering the fearful side of life: what makes the heart pound, the adrenaline flow, the pulse throb, the breath catch in the throat. And hoping always that the reader is having a frightfully good time, too."

Diane Hoh grew up in Warren, Pennsylvania. Since then, she has lived in New York, Colorado, and North Carolina, before settling in Austin, Texas. "Reading and writing take up most of my life," says Hoh, "along with family, music, and gardening." Her horror novels include: *Funhouse*, *The Accident*, *The Invitation*, *The Fever*, and *The Train*.

Point Horror

Are you hooked on horror? Are you thrilled by fear? Then these are the books for you. A powerful series of horror fiction designed to keep you quaking in your shoes.

Titles available now:

The Cemetery
by D.E. Athkins

The Dead Game
Mother's Helper
by A. Bates

The Cheerleader
The Return of the Vampire
The Vampire's Promise
Freeze Tag
The Perfume
The Stranger
by Caroline B. Cooney

April Fools
The Lifeguard
Teacher's Pet
Trick or Treat
by Richie Tankersley Cusick

Camp Fear
My Secret Admirer
Silent Witness
The Window
by Carol Ellis

The Accident
The Invitation
The Fever
Funhouse
The Train
by Diane Hoh